Passion to Survive

Addie Herrington

Passion to Survive
Copyright © 2022 by Addie Herrington

All rights reserved.
No part of this book may be stored in a retrieval system, used or reproduced in any form whatsoever, electronic or mechanical without written permission from the publisher. The only exception is in the case of brief quotations used in critical articles and reviews printed in a newspaper, magazine, or journal.

Published by Kannyn Books
Printed in the United States of America
ISBN-13: 978-1-7326864-9-6

First Edition

Dedication

To James Donnelly, my friend, my therapist, and the man who never gave up on me. As promised, my first book is dedicated to you. I miss you Jim, and even though you left this world, you will always be in my heart, and now you'll be immortal in print.

Acknowledgements

First and foremost, to my editor and husband, James Michael. I know, I know, my spelling and syntax are lousy. I couldn't have done this without you. You made sure that this book had proper grammar! I'm lucky to have you. You are my rock. I love you.

To Brett, my son. Thank you for all your counseling and ideas. (The check's in the mail!) You always gave me the push I needed. The red shirts are all you, Sweetheart.

To Angela, my tech girl. I'm so happy you came into my life. Your encouragement and smarts with technology have been never ending. We make a good team. I hope our friendship lasts for years and years.

To Charlotte, my publisher - my first book! I couldn't have done it without you. I loved your special touches; the little hearts added warmth to the book. Thank you.

Finally, to Alicia, my therapist, who introduced me to my publisher. You told me that it is my time and my turn. I think you are right. Thank you.

Table of Contents

Chapter 1......Page 1

Chapter 2......Page 13

Chapter 3......Page 18

Chapter 4......Page 24

Chapter 5......Page 28

Chapter 6......Page 31

Chapter 7......Page 34

Chapter 8......Page 38

Chapter 9......Page 40

Chapter 10....Page 42

Chapter 11....Page 45

Chapter 12....Page 54

Chapter 13....Page 60

Chapter 14....Page 63

Chapter 15....Page 66

Chapter 16....Page 73

Chapter 17....Page 88

Chapter 18....Page 95

Chapter 19....Page 102

Chapter 20....Page 107

Chapter 21....Page 109

Chapter 22....Page 114

Chapter 23....Page 121

Chapter 24....Page 127
Chapter 25....Page 136
Chapter 26....Page 141
Chapter 27....Page 143
Chapter 28....Page 147
Chapter 29....Page 158
Chapter 30....Page 161
Chapter 31....Page 168
Chapter 32....Page 176

Passion to Survive

Chapter 1

Time to move again. She should have been a pro at it by now, after moving twelve times in six years, but it still upset her. It would have been nice to know she belonged somewhere. Instead, she had to keep looking over her shoulder to see if he was there. She wasn't sure what brought her to Conway, South Carolina, just a feeling that it was safe. Now that feeling was gone.

The next day would be Abby Rineheart's twenty-fourth birthday. It would have been nice to just sit back with a glass of wine and watch a movie. There was no time for that. The hairs on the back of her neck were standing up—she knew he was in the area. Leo Jackson was near. It was time to call Carl.

Carl Pearlman was Abby's estate manager. He was in his late 50s, and stood about 5' 10". He was a thin man, and was balding with a comb-over. He had brown eyes and mousy brown hair.

"Mr. Pearlman's office. May I help you?"

"Hi, Julia, it's Abby. Is Carl in?" Abby asked.

"Hi Abby! How you doing, honey?" Julia asked with concern.

"Hangin' in there," Abby replied with a sigh.

"Well, hang on a minute more while I get Carl. He'll be glad to finally hear from you. It's been close to a year since we heard from you. Are you coming back to Pittsburgh? I'd love to see you again, honey. If you need a place to crash, you know our door is always open."

"Thanks, Jules, I know, but I still don't feel safe in the 'burg. Maybe someday I won't have to worry about it."

"Still running, sweetheart? Come home, let us help you. You know Carl will do everything he can to keep that nut job away from you. Carl isn't just your estate manager;

he loves you like a daughter, as do I."

"I know. He's close again, Jules. I can feel him. How did he get away with killing my mom and dad? It may have been deemed a car accident, but I know dad wouldn't have been on that side of town to begin with, especially with mom. Something just doesn't add up. I don't want to bring this to your door step."

"Carl's here; please call more often, Abby. We worry about you," Julia replied, then handed the phone to Carl.

Abby noticed she didn't really answer her question.

"Abby, are you okay? Where are you?"

Abby heard the concern in his voice.

"Carl, I know that Leo Jackson is close. I sense him. I need money to move again."

"When are you going to quit running? Come home. We will protect you. He can't do anything to you if you are with me," Carl said. "Won't you at least give me an address of where you are at? I can send someone to come and get you."

"I'm not ready yet. One more year and then you won't have to worry about me, anymore. I'll be in charge of my inheritance on my own, and then you will be off the hook."

"I'll always worry about you. I promised your mom and dad that if anything happened to them that I would look out for you. I'll send you what you need for now, but please consider coming back home."

"Thank you, Carl. I will think about it. I'll be in touch."

Carl Pearlman was her father's best friend all through college. They went to the same classes together until her dad started to specialize in medical technology. Carl went on to study law. Her father graduated and advanced in the medical field in specialized technology. He made millions. Although Carl and her father remained friends, Carl struggled in the beginning, until he was able to establish his own practice. He never quite made the millionaire status that his best friend did, but still did quite well for himself.

Abby knew that this move would be the hardest. She had finally met someone that she was more than interested in and was hoping that the relationship would develop into something lasting. Jason Donahue was six years older than her. His family owned a construction business, and it was obvious that he worked a lot outdoors. At six foot two, his muscular tan body could melt a woman. He had jet black hair, pulled back with a leather tie, and ice blue eyes. Abby's dream man.

Jason's company was doing the renovations to the apartment complex where Abby lived. His company had been working there for the past six months and would probably be there six more. Every day, Abby would look out her window and wait for Jason to take his lunch break. As soon as she saw him, she would run out with iced tea in hand and sit with him. As the weeks went by, his lunch breaks became longer; no matter though, he was the boss. He soon looked forward to her company, and they both spent that time getting acquainted. He did ask her out a couple of times. Both times it was just for after work to catch a quick bite. Both times he walked her to her door and gave her a kiss that curled her toes.

Jason was to meet her that night for the third time. It was an official date. She didn't know where he was taking her. He said it was a surprise, and for her to dress comfortably. She just hoped it went well and that they didn't bump into Leo. With all the talks that the two of them had over the months, she stayed clear of her personal past by always changing the subject when he tried to bring it up. Abby was afraid of scaring Jason off before they even had a chance of getting together.

Only an hour to go before the date and she still didn't have anything picked out to wear.

"Jeans it is," she said out loud to herself.

They fit her slight curvy form nicely, hanging on her hips and leaving her flat stomach exposed. A satin blue short top that hugged her full breasts went well and gave a little upscale look. She wore her favorite black high heel boots to finish the ensemble. High heels were her favorite;

they gave height to her five foot four frame.

"Now for this hair," she looked in the mirror and shook her head. Her hair hung to her waist in soft blonde curls. Her green eyes sparkled. She was excited about being with Jason. "I'll just let it hang. The more natural, the better. That's what mom always said."

Just then her doorbell rang.

She left her bedroom and headed to the front door. She opened it, looked up and froze. Jason leaned against the door frame with a confident and sexy smile and said, "Can I come in?"

He wore a black tight tee shirt with snug fitting jeans. She could make out every lean muscle in his body from head to toe, and that's just what Abby did. Her chin dropped and her eyes nearly popped out of her head. This was a far cry from his work overalls. The two previous dinner dates they had were right after work at a nearby fast food joint. This was the first time she had seen him in something other than work clothes.

She didn't realize that she was gawking and not answering him, so Jason gently touched her arm and quietly said, "Abby, can I come in?"

"Oh, sorry! Yes, come on in," she replied blushingly. "You clean up pretty good. Would you care for a beer or glass of wine? I also have iced tea."

"A beer would be great."

She directed him to the living room and told him to make himself comfortable while she got their drinks. He already knew the layout of her apartment; it was one of the ones that he helped build. As she turned, heading toward the kitchen, she looked over her shoulder and caught a glimpse of his butt and walked into the wall with a thud. Jason quickly turned around and went to her.

"Are you okay?" he asked with a grin. He knew he had her flustered.

"I guess I'm a little nervous. I don't have people over much. In fact, you're the first visitor I have ever had here."

"Well, how about this. Why don't we stay here, since it is raining to beat hell, have our drinks and watch a little television? If it quits raining, we can go out to eat later, or if not, we can order in?"

"That sounds great."

She felt comfortable with him thanks to the months of long lunch breaks.

Jason sat on the couch. He patted the cushion next to him and said, "Come and sit down beside me. Maybe the drink will settle you down some. Meanwhile, we can relax a bit."

Abby sat down beside him and proceeded to reach out to the coffee table to grab the remote. Jason gently put his hand on hers and slowly smoothed it up her arm to her neck. He looked into her eyes and leaned in and kissed her gently but fully on the mouth. She shivered. He kissed her again more firmly while threading his fingers through her hair. She kissed him back while his tongue forced its way into her mouth.

"I have been waiting months to do that," Jason said. "Your hair is so beautiful. It feels like silk. I am dying to touch you all over."

Abby's eyes were as big as saucers. She stared at him not knowing what to say or do next. She reached up bravely and touched his cheek, then leaned in and kissed him on the lips. He gently nipped at her lower lip.

"I haven't been with anybody for years. I really don't know what to do next," she said breathlessly.

Jason proceeded to lower her onto the couch, reached up to slide his hand behind her head, and leaned down to lavish her mouth with another devouring kiss. Abby raised her arm to pull on the tie that held his hair back. She had been itching to touch it. His hair came loose. She ran her fingers through it while moving her other hand down his neck and shoulder under his shirt. Jason pulled back.

"Honey, it has been a long time for me also. If we don't move to the bedroom soon, it will be over before we start. Are you on any kind of protection, like the pill?"

"I haven't had a period in over six months. At my doctor visit last week, the doctor said that I wouldn't ovulate again until my stress levels came down and I put on a little weight. He said as long as I was like this, I couldn't get pregnant."

He could feel his zipper pressing against his rock hard cock and feared it could leave a permanent mark. Just thinking of impaling her to the hilt and doing it bare back had him leaking in his jeans. He had never had sex without a condom. He sat up, took a deep breath and asked if they could continue in the bedroom. She smiled and proceeded to her bedroom with Jason close behind.

"Undress for me," she said softly, as she started to undress herself.

By the time she had all her clothes off and was sitting on the end of her bed, Jason was standing in all his glory in front of her with his erection bobbing and straining. She stared up at him and slowly lowered her eyes taking in his firm, tan body. She continued down to his steel hard cock and her eyes widened as she wondered if something that long and thick could even fit inside her. She gasped and looked back up at him.

"Don't worry, sweetheart. It will fit. I'll take it real slow," Jason replied, upon seeing the worry in her eyes.

Abby proceeded to lie on the bed, and pulled herself up on her back until she hit the pillows. He went to the side of the bed and leaned down to cup her face with his hand and his dick touched the side of her thigh. He jumped back up and grabbed the head of his cock with his thumb and forefinger. He pinched it closed to keep from ejaculating right then and there.

"Give me a minute, honey. You look so hot lying naked in front of me. I'm afraid I can't make any promises the first time. Just touching you is making me crazy. You are more beautiful than I even imagined. I'll try to take it slow."

"Just kiss me. You are doing the same thing to me," Abby said as she trembled.

She could feel her clit swelling and her juices making her wet. Her pussy glistened with her arousal. It had been way too long since she was intimate with anyone.

He reached down and slowly ran his hand up her leg. Her skin was so soft he could barely stand it. She spread her legs as he stood at the side of the bed running his hand up to her pussy. He then separated her folds and felt her wetness. He could smell her arousal. That's all it took. He climbed on top of her as slowly as he could, but as soon as his cock hit her entrance, he shook all over and drove his dick in. She felt so warm, wet and good. He looked into her eyes and saw her excitement. Sweat was already forming on his forehead and chest as he grit his teeth to keep from coming.

"Ahh, shit. Abby, I can't hold back. Baby, you feel too good," Jason claimed as he talked through gritted teeth. All control was out the window. He knew he was a goner. "Fuck, you're so tight and hot," he said with a groan.

"Don't hold back. I'm right with you," Abby said.

Air seemed to struggle to reach her lungs. She could feel every vein in his throbbing erection, as she bucked up to meet each thrust. His huge cock reached every sensitive muscle in her aching pussy. All that could be heard in the room was groaning and smacking of flesh as Jason was speeding up. His balls were smacking the cheeks of her ass, and both of them were gasping for air.

"Fuck, Abby! I can't hold out. I'm going to come," Jason speeded up and gave three more hard thrusts then stilled. He shot his release up in her as she called out his name with a loud groan.

He could feel her pussy throbbing with the after effects of her orgasm. He didn't want to move, and neither did she. Both their heartbeats were rapid, so he just held her until they settled a bit. He looked down at her and smiled. She smiled back. When he pulled out of her, he was already semi-erect.

"Sweetheart, that went a little faster than I really wanted it to," Jason said as he rubbed his hand on her belly and proceeded to reach for her breast. "Let me make love to you, slowly."

"Want to take a shower together first? We can see what develops from there," she said with a flirtatious smile.

As she turned her head to the side to look at Jason, she felt his erection throb against her.

"I think we better move before we don't make it out of bed."

He smiled back at her then headed to the bathroom to get the water running. She followed right behind so she could stare at his firm ass. She wanted to reach up and take a squeeze, so she did. He turned and grabbed her into a firm hug. He planted a kiss on her lips while pushing her mouth open and exploring her mouth and taste, again.

"Shower's ready. Let me soap you up," he said as he climbed in and extended his hand to her.

"Only if I can do the same," Abby replied

"Deal," Jason answered.

He grabbed the soap and rag, and lathered up. Starting with her back, he washed her gently, gliding over her lush ass, down each leg and back up to her pussy. Taking his time there, he dropped the rag and continued with his fingers. Turning her to face him, he leaned down and grabbed one of her firm, full breasts with his hand then placed the nipple in his mouth and sucked and nibbled on the tip until it stood straight out. She gave a sigh and a shiver. When he went to the other breast, she reached down and gently grabbed his cock and started to rub her hand up and down feeling the velvety skin over steel.

"Ahhh, honey, damn it to hell," Jason said as he turned her around to face the shower wall, "Place your hands on the wall. I'm going to take you again, right now."

She was hoping he'd say that, because she couldn't seem to get enough of him either. She could feel her clit swelling and her pussy throbbing as he spread her legs and slowly slid his engorged cock into her. They both groaned. He slowly eased in and out, a few times, trying his best to hold on and not lose his control.

"Jason, I need you to go faster. Pinch my nipples. Please. I'm so close to the edge!"

Jason started to thrust faster as he reached around with both hands and cupped both her breasts. He then took her nipples with his thumbs and forefingers and pinched.

Abby let out a scream, and started to buck back onto his cock.

"Fuck, damn, honey hold on. Ahhhh…….shit!" Jason started pounding into her. His balls were tight as they slapped against her. He knew he wasn't going to last. So much for being slow and gentle. He'd be lucky if he'd last until she finished coming. Abby arched her back and groaned out his name, as her pussy grabbed his cock with her orgasm. With a loud groan, Jason stilled as he shot his seed into her, spurt after spurt.

They both stood there weak in the knees, as the water started to cool.

"Baby, I think we should get out before we freeze," Jason said in between gulps of air.

He reached around and turned off the shower. He got out first and hurried and dried himself, then reached for another towel and wrapped Abby up in it. He grabbed her hand and helped her out, then picked her up and carried her into the bedroom.

Abby sat on the edge of the bed, completely sated, looked up at Jason with big eyes and said, "I'm hungry, but I don't want to go out anywhere."

"Yeah, I bet you are hungry. I gave you quite a work out. I hope I didn't hurt you," Jason said as he leaned down to rub the side of her face with the back of his hand. "You are so beautiful. I have dreamt of this for so long, but seeing you and feeling you was so overwhelming that my control was shot."

"You didn't hurt me. I was so excited, I couldn't slow down myself," Abby said, as her cheeks flushed under his soft caress. "I guess this means we'll have to do this again until we get it right."

"With plenty of practice, I think we'll get it right," he said with a grin, "but for now, I better feed you before you collapse on me. How about I order a pizza for delivery?"

"Sounds good to me," she said with a content grin.

They sat at the kitchen table, ate, drank beer, and talked about Jason's past and his family. She learned that before he went into the Air Force, he was once engaged to his childhood sweetheart. Their plans were to marry as soon as his term was up. He said she wrote to him faithfully every day, until one day the letters stopped. Then his parents contacted him to let him know that she had died of an aneurism. It was quick. He was devastated, so he volunteered to take a tour in Afghanistan, not caring if he lived or died. After a year there, his family contacted him again to let him know that his father was getting too old to keep up with the business. They asked him to come home and take over. He decided he had enough and wanted to go home to help out, so his father could retire. When his time was up, he came home and relieved his dad.

Jason went on to say that he had a younger sister. They were born and raised there in South Carolina. His parents were retired and lived near the beach. His little sister, Debbie, was divorced with two kids. She also lived close by. On Sundays, when possible, they all tried to get together at mom and dad's for a Sunday cookout. He mentioned that when she felt ready, he would like her to come with him to meet everyone. Abby was touched that he wanted to include her in his family gathering.

As they were talking, Abby felt like someone was staring at her. She turned her head to look out the kitchen window and saw a face looking back at her. She gasped and jumped.

"Abby, what's wrong? Are you choking?"

Jason jumped up and crossed the table to kneel by her side.

"I looked out the kitchen window and saw a face looking back at me!" She was visibly shaken.

"I'll go out and look around. Lock the door behind me. If there is someone there, honey, I'll find him."

As soon as Jason left, she locked the front door. As she waited, she wondered, was that Leo? Should she run? Should she tell Jason about her past? Every time Jason asked about her family, she changed the subject and turned the conversation back to him. She could tell that he knew what she was doing. It was only a matter of time before he would insist on her revealing whatever he felt she was hiding. Abby was afraid to tell Jason about her family. She was afraid it would push him away. Who in their right mind would want to get involved in such a mess?

There was a light knock on the door.

"Abby, honey, it's me. Let me in," Jason said loud enough for her to hear.

She slowly opened the door to see that it was indeed just Jason and let him in. He gave her a hug.

"Are you okay? Honey, I looked all around the building. Whoever was there is long gone. Did you recognize the face? Was it someone you know?"

"Maybe I just thought I saw a face," she said, as she put her head down.

"Abby, what aren't you telling me? What has you so upset? I don't scare easily. You can talk to me. I won't run away," Jason said softly.

He held her and rubbed his hand up and down her back. He could see that she was still shook up.

"It's not your problem. I don't want to get you involved in it. I can deal with it."

"What is "it? Are you in some kind of trouble? Tell me so I can help you," Jason said softly while he held her.

Jason gently lifted her chin with his fore finger and said, "Baby, you are visibly shaken. Why don't we go cuddle under the covers. I can spend the night. It is late, anyhow, and tomorrow is Sunday. You need some sleep. We can talk some more in the morning."

"Thank you. I like that idea."

They climbed into bed naked. Abby rested her head on Jason's chest, and he hugged her close to him. It wasn't long before he could hear the steady breathing that let him know that she had fallen asleep. He knew she was exhausted. He could see it in her eyes. Jason wondered what she was into. He knew little about her other than she traveled a lot and liked to take pictures. He had some friends on the local police force. Maybe it was time to call in a few owed favors. If Abby was in trouble, he wanted to help. There was just something about her that made him want to protect her. Already he was having feelings for her that he swore he'd never allow himself to feel again. Looking down at her angelic face while she slept on his chest made his heart flutter.

"Oh shit. I'm in trouble," he thought.

He shut his eyes and eventually went to sleep.

Chapter 2

Abby awoke and was surprised by two things - one, that she slept through the night, something she hadn't done since before her parents' deaths, and two, that there was an erection throbbing against her back. She turned her head and smiled at Jason.

"Sorry about that sweetheart. It has a mind of its' own. Having your warm naked body with that soft, lush ass tucked against it doesn't help much," Jason said as he turned her around and planted a tender kiss to her mouth.

He then slowly ran his hand over her belly and up to her breast and cupped it. Massaging it slowly, then pinching the nipple between his thumb and forefinger, he kissed her again. Abby grabbed his penis and started to rub up and down slowly, as she licked and kissed his chest. She then grabbed one of his nipples with her teeth and gave a light bite. He shivered. She proceeded to kiss down to his flat stomach. She turned her head a little to look up at him and saw that his eyes were shut and his head was starting to lean back. So, she continued to work her way down until she gently took her tongue and licked the pre-cum off the head of his cock. He gave a groan.

"Abby, sweetheart, are sure you want to do this?" Jason said, with heat and lust in his eyes.

"I want to see how you taste," she replied with a slight grin.

Taking her tongue and slowly licking around the head of his cock was making her more excited and adventurous. While still lazily rubbing with one hand up and down the shaft, her tongue licked the edge of the head. She then lowered her hand to cup his balls and caressed them. He gave a groan. Her tongue licked down the shaft and back up again.

"Abby, you're killing me. Stick my cock in your mouth," he said desperately.

She looked up at him and smiled. Keeping eye contact with him, she lowered slowly and hovered over the head with her mouth open. He couldn't wait any longer, and with his hips, he pushed his cock into her mouth. She sucked hard and felt the veins in the shaft and the head start to swell more. He held her head gently and started to fuck her mouth. She took him all the way down, then swallowed.

"Fuck! That feels so good, baby. If you don't want me to cum in your mouth, you better stop now," he said, as he looked at her with lust in his eyes.

Abby swallowed again, and when he tried to pull her off of him, she continued to suck up and down. He again grabbed her head. She allowed him to fuck her mouth. He started pumping faster as he was hissing between his teeth. He didn't want it to end so fast; her mouth was so warm and soft. His jaw clenched as she sucked harder. He groaned, and that made her wet and her pussy swell.

"Ahhh…shit, damn, baby, I'm going to come," Jason said through gritted teeth.

He held her head still and pumped with a fury. His groans excited her so much that she wedged her clit against his thigh and humped as she sucked. When she climaxed, she groaned onto his dick, which set him over the edge. She felt the first spurt hit the back of her throat and just kept swallowing. He shot again and again, and she kept up with him. Finally he stiffened his body. He gave a final pump and shot into her mouth. He lay limply on the bed and she licked the rest of his release off the head of his cock.

He reached down and pulled her into his arms next to him. He hugged her close, as he smoothed his hand up and down her back.

"Baby, that was fantastic! It was the best blow job I ever had in my life. You are amazing."

They just rested, cuddling and sighing.

Abby looked up at him and said, "Would you like me to make you some breakfast? I make a pretty mean omelet."

"That sounds great. I can help. Let's get dressed. While we are cooking we can discuss what you would like to do for the day. Unless you are planning on throwing me out after we eat," Jason said, while giving her a pouting look.

"I don't want you to get sick of me," Abby said looking up at him. "You can stay as long as you like. Actually, it is kind of nice to have someone to talk to and do things with."

After they were done eating and cleaning up, Jason suggested that they could spend some time at the beach. He knew a good spot that wasn't very crowded. So, they packed a picnic lunch and headed to the ocean.

The sky was as blue as the water, and the sun shone brightly. It was a beautiful day. As they walked across the sand with their things in tow, Abby kept looking over her shoulder. They picked out a spot and laid out a huge blanket to lie on. Stretching out on the blanket, Abby laid on her stomach and Jason on his back right beside her, drinking up the sun. There was a slight breeze and the easy roll of the ocean waves.

Jason put his hands behind his head and looked up at Abby, "Why do you keep looking over your shoulder? Who are you looking for or running from?"

Abby put her head down and said, "I didn't tell you anything about my past, because I didn't want to scare you away."

"I don't scare easy. Why don't you give me a chance? Maybe I can help you. I do have some connections. Abby, talk to me. I know you are scared of something or someone. I can't help you unless you let me in."

Jason reached over and pulled her close to him. She laid her head on his chest. They stayed that way for a while and just held each other. Jason ran his hand up and down her back soothingly. He patiently waited for her to speak.

Abby raised her head and looked straight into Jason's eyes and said, "When I was seventeen, I lost both my parents. Supposedly they died in a car accident."

"What do you mean, supposedly?"

"My dad's car was found on the wrong side of town. I know my dad would have never taken my mom there. Also, my father's best friend, Carl, told me that the brakes had been messed with, and that he thinks it was done by a man named Leo Jackson. Carl gave me a picture of him, and told me to stay clear of him. He said he is a dangerous man. After I graduated from school, I left town. Leo seems to be following me where ever I go. I can actually feel when he gets close. When I feel him, I leave town and move someplace else. I have been running ever since."

"Do you think that is who you saw in the window last night?"

"I can't be sure. He had a hoodie on. I'm pretty sure, though. I have felt him in the area for a while now."

"Abby, honey, don't be running out on me now. Why don't you come and stay at my house for a while. It's a big place and I have the best security system on the market. You could have your own space and bathroom," Jason asked with hopeful eyes.

"I don't know. I really don't want to impose."

"You would be imposing by running instead, because I would have to come and find you. That would throw my business schedule and clients off, making everyone pissed and costing tons of money and delays."

"Since you put it that way," Abby said shyly, "I would feel better not being alone for a change. I insist on paying rent though."

"You know what could help me out instead of rent?" Jason said with a twinkle in his eye.

"What?"

"You had mentioned that you have had some accounting and filing experience. My books are a mess. I just don't have time in the office to take care of my paper work. You would be doing me a huge favor if you could straighten it all out. You could make your own hours, and it would include your rent plus a decent salary. What do you say?" He stared at her with his big ice blue eyes with so much hope in them; he knew he'd win her over.

"How can I resist an offer like that? When do you want me to start?"

"Yesterday! Let's go back to your place and get your things," Jason said as he stood up and started gathering everything. "On the way back, I have to stop at my office to go over some things with the crew. You may as well come with me and meet everyone. That way you will be familiar with everybody."

After spending a couple hours at Jason's office, they drove back to Abby's apartment. Since it was a furnished, one-bedroom, the only things to pack were her personal items, clothing, and a few odds and ends. Jason said that he knew the owner of the complex, since he had been remodeling the place, and he'd finish tying things up for her. While they were packing, Abby asked about the guys in his crew and what they were like. The men had been very polite to her and made her feel welcome, except the new guy, he just stared at her a lot.

Chapter 3

She had never been to Jason's house before. When they pulled into his driveway, she just sat in her car, which was behind Jason's truck, and stared. His place was huge. It had a wrap-around porch with a swing in front. She noticed a three-car garage, all brick that had two stories. Even the stone steps leading up to the porch were wide and impressive. The property itself was beautiful. She could see that the back was a wooded area, and that there was a large pond to one side. The place was definitely secluded.

She jumped when he tapped on her window. "Are you going to get out, or just sit there all day?" he asked smiling at her.

She opened her door and said, "Your place is so beautiful! I had no idea that it would be so big."

"I'm glad you like it. I designed and built it myself in the hopes that someday I'd have a family to fill it. Come on. Leave your stuff; let me show you around first. I'll bring your stuff in later."

He grabbed her hand and led her inside. She stood in the foyer. Her chin dropped as she slowly looked around. The place was awe inspiring. The huge living room had a brick fireplace against the side wall with a mantle surrounding it. A huge bay window took up just about the whole front wall and gave an impressive view of the front of the property.

"Come on. I'll show you around," he said smiling. She still was not believing she was really there.

He showed her the three extra bedrooms, and told her she could have her pick. She picked the room farthest from the master bedroom, thinking she wanted to make sure he had his own privacy. After he brought up all her things and set them in her room, he took her hand and led her into the master bedroom. She stopped and looked at the immense bed. It was, as all the other furniture in the room, a dark rich mahogany. It had four posts with a very heavy headboard. The bed spread was a warm, maroon velvet with just enough pillows to make it comfortable, yet manly.

"This is where I hope you spend most of your nights, with me," he said softly. "Consider this your home. I hope you are here for a long time, but that will be entirely up to you. I know things are moving kind of fast. I just don't want you to run. If you let me in to what is going on with you, I will do my best to make you feel safe. You look so overwhelmed, honey. Talk to me. What can I do to make you comfortable?"

She was still staring at the bed. How did this just happen? One minute Jason was going to take her out on a date, the next minute she is moving in with him. Is it possible to find a true mate that quickly? She felt safe with him. He was so gentle and loving towards her, but what if Leo found her? What if he tried to hurt Jason? She could never forgive herself if something happened to him.

"Abby, sweetheart, you look like you are frozen in one spot. What is going on in that pretty head of yours? You have me worried. Talk to me," he said as he rubbed his hand up and down her back.

She slowly looked up at him and said, "That's a big bed!"

He smiled and gave her a big hug.
"Let's go down to the kitchen and I'll show you where everything is. If you want, I'll whip up some supper, and we can sit in front of the fireplace and talk."

She didn't say anything. She just let him lead her to the kitchen. The kitchen was a woman's dream. It had all the modern appliances. There was an island in the center with a spare sink. Copper pots and pans hung from the ceiling in order, all shiny and new. She wondered if he did any real cooking. That was something she always wanted to do, but was too busy running in survival mode. It would be nice to relax for once. It made her heart heavy just thinking about it. She could see herself living here a long time with Jason, and she dreamed as the sun shone through the kitchen window lighting up the whole room.

"What are you dreaming about, honey?" Jason asked. "You seem like you are in a different world. Here, why don't you look through the fridge and see if there is something you would like. We can cook up something together."

"I'd like that. Of course, I have to warn you, my cooking skills are kind of lacking. I have never been in one place long enough to really learn how."

"That's okay. Between the two of us, I think we won't poison each other," he said with a boyish grin. He gave her a playful tap on her butt.

After supper, while sitting on the couch, Abby just stared at the fireplace. Jason could see the worry in her face.

"A penny for your thoughts," he said softly as he placed his hand over hers.

"What if things don't work out?"

"How will we know if we don't give it a try? Abby, we have been actually seeing each other for months now. I'm not exactly some stranger to you. I can and want to take care of you and make you feel safe. We'll take it a day at a time," Jason said. "Tell ya what. Take a few days and just get acquainted with the house. When you feel ready, I'll bring you into my office and you can start working. A few more days of my paperwork in shambles isn't going to make much difference."

"Are you sure about that? I really could use a day or two to sort things out."

"Sweetheart, I'm so happy you are here. If need be, you could even do the work at home. You let me know what you need to feel comfortable," Jason said as he reached for her arm and pulled her up next to him. "Come with me. I want to show you something."

Jason led her to the master bathroom. There was a glass wall that viewed the landscape of the back of the house. Off to the side was a huge hot tub that had steps leading into it.

Abby took in a deep breath, "Oh Jason, this is just beautiful! Can we get in now?"

"That's why I brought you in here. I knew you'd like it. I'll start the hot water while you undress," he said, while he wiggled his eyebrows and grinned.

While smiling back, she quickly disrobed and started removing his clothes as he was testing the water. They both stepped in. He sat against the tub and pulled her in between his legs with her back up against him. The tub was big enough to fit six people. He turned the jets on, and she just sighed deeply. While they relaxed, Jason reassured her that everything would work out, and that in time, she would see that.

Having her up against him, naked and soft, was driving him crazy. All he could think about was fucking her, being in her, and driving them both wild. His penis was thinking the same thing and was fully erect, throbbing up against her lower back. After a while, he gently reached up and cupped her breasts. She leaned back so she could kiss his lips. With his thumb and forefinger, he gave both her nipples a pinch that sent a shock straight to her pussy. She groaned out loud then reached behind her and grabbed his thick, hard cock with one hand and surprised him when she raised herself up and guided his cock into her swollen pussy.

"Ahhh…fuck, baby, you feel so damn good. So fucking tight! You are going to be the death of me," Jason growled as he lowered his hands to grasp her waist. "Let me fuck you. I'll lift you."

He slowly lifted her up and down like she didn't weigh a thing. Between the jets and the whirlpool caused by the up and down action, Abby was lost in sensation. He started to increase his speed lifting her. She could feel every vein in his shaft as his cock head swelled up even more. Their breathing and groaning was getting faster and louder. Jason continued his grip on her waist, lifting her like she was his own personal blow up doll. The swooshing water was starting to hit the floor.

"Baby, are you close? I don't know if I can hold on any longer," Jason asked breathily. "You feel so good. Your pussy is grabbing me like a vice." He was taking in a breath, hissing through gritted teeth to keep from coming.

Abby knew she was close, so she took her finger and started to rub her clit. With a deep breath she called out his name, "Jason, go faster, harder!"

"Fuuuck, I'm coming, ahhhh shit,"
He held her hips down and fucked her harder as he increased his speed. He rose up with one final push and spilled in her pussy. His release was all it took to send Abby over the edge into a mind blowing climax. His body jerked with each shot of cum, once, twice, the third time he held still inside her as far as he could, until every last spurt of his seed was released. He held her tight and could feel both their hearts beating fast. He knew then that he was falling in love with her.

Abby didn't have the strength to move. Every muscle in her body felt liquid. She just lye back against Jason's chest and he hugged her while still inside her, not wanting to move himself. They both sat there for quite a while, listening to the whirling water coming out of the jets.

"I'm afraid we are going to turn into prunes if we don't get out," Jason said in a soft low voice. "I'll lift you up and forward, sweetheart. Let me get out first then I'll help you out."

When he lifted her up off his cock, they both gave out a groan.

There were no arguments from Abby. She was so content and sated. After he dried off, he grabbed a towel, threw it over his shoulder, then reached down and picked her up in his arms. After he set her down on the bath chair, he dried her off and carried her to bed. Her head no sooner hit the pillow than she was out like a light.

Jason slowly crawled in beside her and spooned her ass against him. Laying his arm around her waist, he tucked her in closer. He rested his chin in her head taking in the sweet smell of her while listening to her steady breathing. His thoughts went back to when he was in the service nearly ten years before. He pushed that one day out of his mind for so long, it surprised him when it crept in again. The day when he got the call that Michelle, his fiancé died.

Michelle was his childhood sweetheart. They had grown up together and the families knew that they would someday be married. Jason and Michelle had set the date for when he returned from his time in the service. She had written to him every day, until one day the letters stopped coming. A few days later, his parents contacted him and told him that she had died from a brain aneurism. He was devastated. Truth be told, he elected to go to Afghanistan feeling that it really didn't matter anymore if he lived or died.

After spending over a year overseas, he was given the option to come back home, so he did. His dad needed him to take over the family construction business, because he wanted to retire. Working helped to keep his mind off of Michelle. After five or six years, he did date a few times, but no one kept his interest until the day he saw Abby.

As he lye there with Abby, he hugged her gently, not wanting to wake her. He never thought he would fall in love again, but he did, and he'd be damned if he let anyone or anything happen to her. He would protect her with his life, and thank God every day that she came into his life.

Chapter 4

Monday morning, neither one of them wanted to get up, but Jason knew he had to go to the office early, so he could head out with his crew. Abby got up with him and made him some breakfast, while he got ready to leave for the day. She even packed him a lunch. It felt good, almost like she was finally home and belonged. She didn't want it to end.

"Sweetheart, will you be okay here alone?" Jason asked, as he gave her a kiss on the forehead.

"I'll be fine. I need to settle in anyhow. My stuff is still in boxes," she said, as she gave him a big hug.

"I put the office number and my cell number on the fridge. Call me if you need me. Call me even if you don't need me. In fact, just call me," he said.

"Go! You'll be late. The guys will be wondering where you are. Who knows, I may even surprise you with an iced tea," she said with a big grin.

"Oooh Baby, you know what I like!" He gave her butt a quick slap and headed out the door.

He went to the office first to give out the assignments for the day, then drove out to the site. As he was checking things out, he looked over at Abby's apartment and saw a man looking in her windows. He had on a hoodie. Jason ran over to see what he wanted. The guy started to run. Jason circled around the opposite way and tackled the man in the back of the building. Pinning him to the ground, Jason turned him over and asked, "Who the hell are you, and what are you doing looking in windows?"

"You're the one who was sitting in Abby's kitchen the other day," the stranger said.

"How do you know Abby?" Jason yelled in his face.

"She's my twin!"

Jason let go of the guy's arms and just looked at him in shock. "He did kind of resemble Abby, same eyes, hair, and facial structure," Jason thought.

Leo stood about six foot, had broad shoulders, and was muscular. Jason would find out later that his fitness was due to having to survive living in the streets. His blonde hair was long and unkempt, curling at his neck.

"She has never mentioned any twin to me. You better start talking," Jason said as he stared at the stranger.

"She doesn't know."

"What do you mean, she doesn't know. How could she not know she has a twin?" Jason said, as he backed up and just stared at the guy.

"If you would let me up, I'll explain."

Jason proceeded to get up. He looked down at the man and asked, "What's your name?"

"Leo Jackson."

"You're the guy who has been chasing Abby. You're the one who killed her parents and got away with it! What do you mean, you are her twin?" Jason was getting angrier by the second.

"I didn't kill her parents - my parents. Jackson is my adopted name. My real last name is Rineheart," Leo continued to explain. "When Abby and I were born, I was kidnapped from the hospital."

Leo went on to explain that he came to find out that the kidnapper was holding him hostage for ransom, but was stabbed in the chest by someone, and the baby, Leo, was left in a box at the broken down row house where the kidnapper had lived. Neighbors heard his cries, and police eventually found him.

He was put up for adoption. The boy went from foster home to foster home, until he ran away and lived in the streets. He managed to live on his own. He decided to find out who he really was by the time he hit his twenties. His street smarts helped him with that, and after he obtained documentation, he looked up his parents, only to find out that they were killed in an auto accident. That's when he learned he had a twin sister.

When Leo investigated further, he found out that his sister was left to the care of a Carl Pearlman. He went to see this Carl, but was thrown out before he could even talk to him. Leo was surprised that Pearlman wouldn't meet with him, especially after he produced proof of who he was. That made him suspicious, so he went on instead to hunt down his sister. He had been following her ever since.

Jason was shocked and stood there running his hand through his hair. He didn't know what to say. How was he going to tell Abby? She was terrified of this guy.

"It has taken me years to find out all this information," Leo said. "I have to talk to Abby - to warn her."

"Warn her of what?"

"I'm not the one she has to worry about. Someone is out to kill her and me. I have had attempts out on me several times. Please, you have to take me to her. I can show both of you proof of everything I've told you. If you care anything about Abby, take me to her," Leo said with desperation in his eyes.

Jason took Leo back to his office and Leo did show Jason legal papers and other medical documents that appeared to prove who he was. Leo explained that every time he got close to Abby, she packed up and ran. He could never get close enough to explain everything to her. When she saw him, she would look at him with fear, and run. He knew then that someone was feeding her lies about him. When he had looked in her kitchen window and saw Jason with her, he felt like that was his first break to get close to her. In all these years, he never saw her with anyone or he would have approached that person, just like he was telling Jason.

"Why did you run from me?" Jason asked.

"Because I didn't recognize you right away," he said, "and someone has been after me as well as Abby. We have to warn her. She is in danger."

Jason grabbed his cell phone to give Abby a call. The phone just rang. He tried the house phone, again no answer.

He looked at Leo and said, "I left her this morning at my house. She was just going to kick back and get used to the place. We better head over there and see why she isn't answering."

Jason jumped into the driver's seat of his truck and told Leo to hop in. His office was only twenty minutes from his house. It was the longest twenty minutes he ever drove.

Chapter 5

When they pulled into his driveway, her car was still parked where she left it. The front door to his house was wide open. Jason's heart pounded. He knew she would never leave it open. They both jumped out and ran to the house. Inside, the entryway was a mess. Things were thrown about. There was blood on the floor. He ran upstairs yelling her name. Her belongings were still setting in her room, untouched. He ran through every room. She was gone. Jason just slid slowly down the foyer wall and sat on the floor, not knowing what to do next. Leo was standing there looking at him. The cell phone in Jason's jean pocket starting ringing.

"Yeah, Dave, what's up?" Jason asked of his foreman. When Jason wasn't on site, he expected Dave to take over and direct the crew. David Hughes was in his fifties, and had been with the business since Jason's dad started the company. He was about 5' 11" with graying temples. He was still in pretty good shape, but had a slight beer gut. A good hearted, honest man, Dave was loyal to the bone.

"That new guy we just hired?"

"Yeah?"

"He didn't come in this morning, and that cell number he gave us is bogus," Dave replied. "Now what, boss?"

"What do we know about the guy?"

"Not much. If you want, I'll sniff around and see what I can find out."

"Yeah, do that," Jason said, still in a fog over Abby.

"Boss, are you going to be here soon, or do you want me to just go ahead with the plans?"

"Dave, I have some personal shit to deal with right now. Go ahead with what we talked about last week. Call me right away if you find anything out about the new guy," Jason said.

"Will do," Dave replied, and then hung up.

As he went to put his cell back in his pocket, Jason noticed Abby's purse under the end table by the living room couch. He knew she never went anywhere without it. He jumped up to get it.

Leo followed right behind. "We got to find her. I was afraid something like this might happen."

"She never would leave the house without her purse," Jason said, as he started to look through it.
Inside it was her cell phone, wallet, some makeup, a brush, and a picture of Leo. He pulled it out and showed to him.

"Where did she get this?" Leo asked.

"She showed it to me the day you looked through her kitchen window," Jason said. "She said that Carl, her guardian, gave it to her and told her to stay away from you, because you killed her parents and that you are extremely dangerous."

"No wonder I couldn't get close to her!" Leo was pissed…and worried.

Leo went on to explain that as he started digging into his birth and kidnapping, he had learned that this Carl Pearlman was an alleged friend of his natural parents. He had never really known the man. After the death of his natural parents had hit the papers and he learned about everything, he made an attempt to meet the guy, but Pearlman refused to see him. That's when he felt that things weren't adding up. He decided to find his twin sister himself and try to find out what was really going on.

"Looks like we need to pay a visit to this Pearlman guy," Jason said as he and Leo headed to his truck. "Wait a minute. Are we going to Pittsburgh?"

"Looks that way," Leo replied.

"I need to pack some stuff and call Dave. This is going to take a couple of days," Jason said.

"At least! All I have is in my backpack. I'm ready when you are," Leo said as he walked to the truck. He knew time could not be wasted, not if they wanted to find his sister alive.

"I knew she was in danger," Leo remarked.

"How did you know?"

"I sensed it. I could feel it," Leo said looking straight at Jason.

"Funny," Jason said looking back at him. "She said something similar about you. She told me that she could sense when you got close to her."

"Must be a twin thing," Leo said to himself, as well as to Jason.

Chapter 6

Carl was readying himself for the next business meeting at his office when his personal cell phone rang.

"Carl here."

"It's Darcy."

"Is the job done?" Carl said anxiously.

"Well there, Carl. There has been a slight change of plans."

"What do you mean by that? Did you find her?"

"Yeah, it took a bit, but I found her. Pretty little thing she is," Darcy replied with a chuckle.

"Finish the job, Darcy, or you won't get paid!"

"This is where the change comes in. While I was working on my plans, I come to find out that our little Abby is worth quite a few million."

"Is she still alive or what?"

"Oh she's alive alright. I have her stashed away nice and safe."

"We had a business agreement! Unless you finish her off, you don't get a dime," Carl growled through gritted teeth.

"Listen up, Carl. This is how it's going to go down. I want two million in my account by the end of the week, or I let our little Abby loose with all the info she will need to end you," Darcy replied. "I'll call you back when I see that you made the transaction." The phone went dead.

"Fuck!" Carl pounded on his desk with his hand tossing papers everywhere. He had no idea what he was going to do now. Transferring the cash wouldn't be too bad of a problem, but what if it didn't stop there? Darcy could drag this out forever, or until he bled him dry.

"Why didn't I just make her come home? Then I could have arranged things here where I had control," Carl said to himself.

Things were a mess. He would have to think fast in

order to get everything under control. Now he would have two murders to deal with. He had to call Sully. He didn't like dealing with Sully, not because he was part of the mob or even that he was a hit man. What Carl didn't like about him was that once he did a job, he would hang around awhile acting like he was your friend. What choice did he have at this point? He wasn't about to give in to Darcy.

"Sully, its Carl," Pearlman said with a sigh.

"Hey, man. What's up?"

"I have a job for you," Carl said without pleasantries. "It's a two-parter."

Jason and Leo crossed the border into Virginia. They had to stop for gas. Jason needed to stretch his legs, anyhow. He realized that he had been gripping the steering wheel until his knuckles were white. For the most part, the two of them had been quiet. Then Jason spoke.

"She had to have known the person," he thought out loud. "I showed her how my security system works. No one could have gotten in unless she let them in. She either knew the person or had reason to trust him."

"Has she been with anybody since she's been with you?" Leo asked.

"Not really. I introduced her to my crew … FUCK! Let's pull into this gas station. You gas up the truck while I give my crew foreman a call."

"Dave here."

"Dave, its Jason. Any news on the new guy?"

"I asked around, and he is new in town. So far, I got nothing. What's up, Jason? You sound anxious."

"Abby is missing. When I got back to my place, the door was open. All her things are still there including her handbag. I think this new guy has something to do with it," Jason said. "We are heading to Pittsburgh to try and get some answers. Keep digging on that new guy Darcy. I'm counting on ya, man."

"Don't worry about things here, boss. I'll keep the crew on schedule, and I'll call you if I find out anything. You just be safe. I hope you find Abby." With that, he hung up.

After filling up the truck, taking care of essentials, they both headed back on the road. Jason wasn't sure where he was going. He had a general idea where this Carl lived from the many talks he had with Abby. He wasn't even sure that Carl would even know anything, but he and Leo felt it was a place to start. All he knew was that he couldn't just sit and do nothing. He had to try and find her. He couldn't even begin to think of being without her. Leo and Jason compared notes of what they both knew in the hope that, somewhere along the line, they would stumble across a clue.

Chapter 7

…………………..♥ ♥…………………..

Somewhere in West Virginia

Abby woke up with a lump on her head and a terrible headache. She ached all over. Her hands were tied behind her back and her ankles were tied together. She was on the floor. She looked around to try and get her bearings. The room was dark and the floor was dirt. There were no windows. It appeared that she was inside of some kind of shed. She noticed some garden tools against one corner. Just then, the door opened and light shown in nearly blinding her.

"Well, look who's awake?" Darcy said with a smirk on his face.

"Why are you doing this? Let me go," Abby said pleadingly, not wanting to anger him. Starting to remember who he was and how he tricked her to let him in Jason's house she said, "Jason will look for me. Let me go before it is too late. I won't even mention you."

"I'm not worried about what he knows. I'll bet Jason, Mr. Boss Man, didn't know what a little golden chickie he had, did he?"

Darcy slowly moved over and knelt down beside her. He took his hand and started to run it down her face and hair. Abby jerked back.

"Pretty little thing aren't you. I'll bet you feel real good under all those clothes." He grabbed her hair and pulled her head up and gritted his teeth. He smiled into her face and said, "Don't piss me off. If things don't go the way I want, then I'll just kill you. If they do, then I'll let you go after I fuck you. I think I'll fuck you either way." He started laughing as he let go of her hair. He reached up her shirt, ripped her bra and squeezed her breast. Abby screamed and pulled away. He just gave her an evil grin and backed out of the shed, closing the door behind him.

Abby shook all over and tears started to fall down her cheeks. How was she going to get out of here? Where is here? Does Jason even know she's gone yet?

"Abby, get yourself together. You have to figure a way out of here," she said to herself.

She looked around, again noticing the tools in the far corner. Maybe she could scoot over and try to find something to cut the duct tape that bound her hands together. She started to wiggle over toward the tools, and spotted a sickle. Turning her back to it, she looped her hands over it, and proceeded to slide them up and down the blade. It was working! It was almost loose when she heard footsteps heading her way. She stopped and wiggled her way back to where she was just in time for Darcy to walk back in. She hoped he wouldn't notice the tear and dirt on her jeans and tee shirt.

"Are you hungry? Have to pee? I'll gladly help you with that."

He was leaning against the door, looking at her like she was a piece of meat. A rich piece of meat.

"No. All I need is for you to let me go. Apparently you know about my parents' money. If you let me go, I can make a call and get you what you want," Abby said, trying to stay calm.

"To who? Carl?" he said laughing.

"How do you know Carl?"

"Who do you think sent me?"

She stared at him in utter horror.

"Why? Why would Carl do this? He was my parents' friend, wasn't he?" Her mind was racing as she tried to figure out all that was happening. If what he was saying was true, then…..

"This isn't the first job he has sent me on," Darcy said, "Since I'm probably going to kill you, there is no skin off my back if I tell you. He had me cut the brakes to your parents' car. I then chased them off the road. He paid me well for that one!"

Abby felt her stomach grow sick. She leaned up and

dry heaved. She realized now that if she didn't get out of here she was going to die before Jason could find her. She turned her head into the dirt floor and just wept.

"Don't cry there little chickie," he said mockingly, "Here, maybe this will cheer you up a bit."

She turned her head and looked up and saw Darcy kneeling right in front of her with his dick bobbing in her face. She gasped and shivered. She screamed with all that was left in her hoping someone, anyone would hear.

"Now, now there little chickie. No need for all this fussing. No one is going to hear you out here in the woods. Just open that pretty little mouth and suck my dick. If you dare to bite me I'll beat you senseless. If you are a good little girl, I may let you live longer. Now open wide," he said as he grabbed her hair and yanked her head onto his dick.

He brutishly pumped into her mouth like he was fucking a well-used whore.

Abby just shut her eyes as tears ran down her cheeks. She could hardly breathe as he pumped viciously into her mouth. She didn't fight him. How could she? Instead she thought about how she would escape when he left. Thank God it didn't take him too long before he let out a groan and shot into her mouth. He pulled out and patted her head. How could Carl do this to her?

"Good girl. I'll let you live a little longer. I still have to fuck you later. You better rest up now, you'll need your strength," Darcy said.

He then got up, opened the door to give his limp dick some air, then stuck it back into his dirty jeans as he continued out the door.

She gagged and tried to throw up. Abby just glared at him as he left. He was a lanky man. She figured he was somewhere in his late forties, dirty looking with gray in his scruffy hair and an unshaven face. His face had scars and skin of leather. He was scary looking. It was so hard to believe that Carl would have anything to do with him.

As he headed out, he turned and looked at her one more time. She shut her eyes and pretended to go to sleep. He just smiled lustily and left.

She listened for his footsteps leaving. Not knowing when he would be back, she hurried and scooted back over to the sickle. It only took a few more pulls on the blade, and her hands were loose. Quickly she untied her ankles. When she stood up, she swayed a bit. Her head throbbed, and blood rolled down her face. Steadying herself, she slowly went to the door. Just opening the door a crack, she noticed that it was dusk, and that there were woods all around her. She didn't see Darcy, anywhere. It was now or never. She darted out the door and headed to the back of the shed, since every time she heard Darcy approach the shed it was from the front.

Running deeper into the woods, she realized it was only a matter of time before Darcy would return and see her gone. She had to get as much distance between them as possible. She heard a stream up ahead and ran toward it. She never realized how thirsty she was, until she started drinking the fresh water. She splashed water on her face and arms to clean herself off as best as possible. Looking up stream, she realized, would take her opposite from the shed, so that's the way she went.

Chapter 8

Sully knocked on Carl's office door, then opened it to let himself in. That was another reason Carl didn't like him. He made himself at home. But, Carl knew he was good at what he did, and that he left nothing behind. Things were getting out of hand with Darcy and Carl knew it. "Time to clean up things a bit," Carl thought to himself.

Sully Marino was a big man - muscled and lean. He looked like the stereotypical Italian hood with his dark brown, slicked back hair and brown eyes. Most times he wore a suit, as he did now. Carl figured he was in his mid-thirties because of his strength and stamina.

"Hey Carl. What can I do for you?" he asked pleasantly with a smile.

"I need you to find someone and dispose of him. He should have a young woman with him, and I need her gone, as well. Have a seat and I'll fill you in."

Carl showed him pictures of both Abby and Darcy. Carl figured that Darcy would be at the old shed in West Virginia. That's where he seemed to end up with all the other jobs he was assigned, the dumb shit. Carl had a general idea where the shed and cabin were, even though he was never there. He knew Sully wouldn't have any problem finding it.

"You know my fee. It will be doubled now, plus expenses," Sully said, business like.

"I'll give you half now and half when the job is done."

"That's fine," he said and stood to shake Carl's hand, "I'll be in touch."

Sully turned and left, closing the door behind him. Carl let out a huge sigh, and yelled for Julia to get him a cup of coffee. He needed to catch up with his case files and knew he was in for a long night. With any luck, he'd get a call saying the job was done.

Julia came in with his coffee and asked, “Was that a new client that just left?”

“Don’t worry about it, honey. If he becomes a client, I’ll let you know. For now it was just an information meeting,” Carl said to her with a smile.

She had no idea what he was up to with a lot of things and he planned to keep it that way, for her own good…and his.

Chapter 9

Jason and Leo crossed over the border into West Virginia. Leo volunteered to drive awhile to give Jason a break. Jason's cell phone went off and he quickly answered it.

"Jason here."

"Hey Jason. Any news yet?" Dave asked.

"No. What about your end?"

"I was talking to the crew," Dave said, "and they said that the other day when you brought Abby by and introduced her to everybody, that Darcy had made some crude comments."

"Like what?"

"You're not going to like this, but he was saying stuff like he bet Abby would be a tasty piece of ass, and that he wouldn't mind fucking some of that," Dave said as humbly as he could.

"That fucking bastard! Did the guys say anything else about him?"

Jason was obviously pissed, and was gritting his teeth.

"Yeah. After the guys were done with their shift, they all went to the local bar. After he had a few, his mouth ran a bit more. The guys said that he claimed that he was going to be rich soon, and that he couldn't wait to get back to his cabin in West Virginia. Sorry about all this, Boss. I had to tell you."

"I know Dave. I don't blame you. In fact, you helped a lot. See if the guys can remember anything else. It would be very helpful to find that damn cabin. We are in West Virginia, now," Jason said as calmly as he could.

"I will. Oh, two more things. His last name is Schmitt, and that cabin is somewhere near Summersville."

"Good work, Dave. Keep in touch and I'll do the same."

Jason disconnected the call and looked at Leo.

"Are you going to fill me in?" Leo asked.

Jason gave him the low down on the conversation with Dave. Leo punched the steering wheel. They both knew that they were running out of time. Abby was in serious danger. They had to pull over, get a bite to eat, and come up with some sort of game plan.

Chapter 10

……………….♥ ♥………………

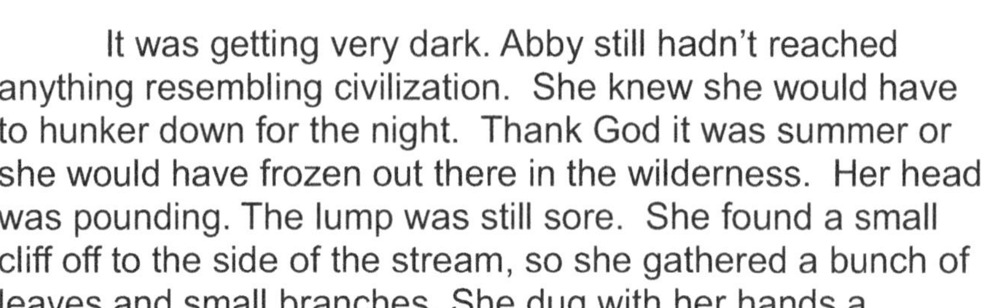

It was getting very dark. Abby still hadn't reached anything resembling civilization. She knew she would have to hunker down for the night. Thank God it was summer or she would have frozen out there in the wilderness. Her head was pounding. The lump was still sore. She found a small cliff off to the side of the stream, so she gathered a bunch of leaves and small branches. She dug with her hands a shallow hole under the cliff, just big enough for her to curl up. She lined the hole with the leaves for warmth, climbed in and curled up into a ball, then took the small branches and leaves to cover herself. No one seemed to be following her.

Rolled up in a ball and snug against the small cliff, she started to think of everything that had happened to her since she opened the front door that morning to let one of Jason's crewmen inside. It was then that she started to silently sob. Streams of tears ran down her cheeks, and she shook violently. How was she to know that Darcy would hurt her? He said that Jason sent him to pick up some diagrams from his home office.

All this time she thought it was just Leo after her. Was it Darcy all along? Her heart was breaking as she ran everything over in her mind, what Darcy said about Carl. Why? Carl was daddy's best friend, wasn't he? Why would he want her dead? Was this all about money? She never paid much attention to her parents' fortune. She knew that they had money, but the amount never mattered much to her. Her parents had always taught her to earn whatever she wanted to have in life.

Her stomach growled and ached. Even though she hadn't eaten since early that morning, she wasn't at all hungry, but she was tired. So very tired. She knew she couldn't stay awake much longer.

Back toward the area that Carl told Sully he could find Darcy's cabin, Sully pulled off the road, and pulled out his highly sophisticated GPS. With it, he believed he could find a small crater on the moon. No one would think that someone like Sully would have that kind of technology. Using it, he brought up the whole area within a five mile radius. Zooming in, he found a deserted looking cabin. Bingo. From there he would have to travel on foot. He gathered up his equipment, along with his long range sniper rifle, hand weapons, various knives, and ammunition, and headed out.

Even though it wasn't dark yet, he could see perfectly with his night vision goggles. Being a sharp shooter in the service taught him how to prepare for damn near anything. He knew he was just a few miles away from the sight, so he hurried ahead. When he was close enough, he scouted around the perimeter of the cabin. He found a good spot that gave clear vision to the front of the cabin and a few feet to the left gave clear vision to the front of the shed. Hiding behind a large tree he saw Darcy coming out of the cabin rubbing his dick through his jeans and heading for the shed. "That sick fuck," Sully said to himself, "he must have the girl tied up in the shed and he's going to do a number on her."

Sure enough he saw Darcy enter the shed. A few minutes later he heard an ungodly scream. He knew it was Abby, had to be. He wanted to save her, but figured he'd only give himself away. After a few minutes Darcy came out of the shed placing his limp dick into his jeans. Sully knew then that she had to have been tied up. That was the only way that ugly mother fucker could have gotten a piece of ass.

Darcy had entered the cabin, and a few minutes later Sully saw the door of the shed start to open and a woman peeked out and looking around. Abby. She looked pretty beat up. Her lips were swollen and she had a nasty lump on her forehead. She then slipped out of the shed and high tailed it to the woods in the back of the shed.

"Fuck," Sully thought. He'd go after her after he took care of Darcy.

When Sully knew Abby was gone, he slowly approached the cabin and peeked into the window. He saw Darcy making a call on his cell. Before he could continue to talk, Sully slowly opened the door finding Darcy aiming his gun, but Sully was quicker and shot Darcy in the head.

He could hear someone on his phone going "Hello?" He knew it was Carl, so he answered, "One down Carl, and one to go."

"Is that you Sully?" Carl asked.

"Yeah. Darcy is dead. Clean head shot. I'll just leave him here. It will be months before anyone finds him, if at all," Sully said.

"What about the girl?"

"I witnessed that Darcy had raped her and beat her up pretty good," Sully said in the hope that Carl would change his mind about the kill.

"Is she there?"

"After Darcy did a number on her, inside the shed, she managed to escape into the woods. I couldn't go after her until I took care of Darcy. Do you still want her down?"

"Take her down. Do it as painlessly as you can."

"Right."

Carl disconnected the call. Sully wasn't in a hurry. He really felt sorry for the girl. He knew that Carl could be cold, but he was surprised how heartless he really was.

He left the cabin and headed back to his vehicle, figuring that Abby couldn't get too far. It was getting dark. She would have to find shelter soon. He wouldn't. He would continue to track her into the night.

Chapter 11

Jason and Leo were sitting at a local diner checking out various maps that were on display. The maps showed the small town they were in and the surrounding area. They decided that the best thing to do was to ask some of the locals if they ever heard of a family named Schmitt that owned a hunting cabin in the woods. It took a while but finally they did find someone that knew Darcy's father.

"Yeah, Schmitty used to bring his kill into town here and have the butcher fillet it. He'd give the butcher damn near half of it in return for payment," an old man recalled as he rocked away on the porch of the diner. "I never liked that S.O.B."

"Do you know where his cabin is?" Leo asked.

"Here, give me that map. I can show you the general area. Schmitty liked his privacy durin' huntin' season."

The old man proceeded to point to the location of the cabin, and told them how they could get there. Both men thanked him and headed out.

"We don't have a lot of daylight left. We better hustle," Jason said as he jumped behind the wheel of his truck.

They went as far as they could in the truck, then parked on the side of a dirt road. The rest of the way had to be done on foot. They packed some gear, water, a couple knives, some food, then Jason asked, "You wouldn't by any chance have a gun, would you?"

Leo smiled and removed his backpack. He pulled out a hand gun. Jason's eyes got wide.

"Don't worry. I have a license to carry it and I know how to shoot. I told you before that several attempts have been made on my life. I had to protect myself."

"We'll talk more about this later. Right now, I'm glad you have it. Let's go find Abby,"

They were running in the woods for about an hour,

stopping only to check the map and look for telltale signs the old man told them to watch for. Looking far in the distance, Jason gave Leo a shove then pointed. There ahead was an old log cabin with a shed off to the side. They slowed down and split up to circle the area and check it out. They met back in front of the cabin a few yards away.

"Did you see anybody or hear anything?" Jason asked Leo.

"No. Did you?"

"No. I'm glad you have a gun. This place doesn't look too welcoming. We better move in slow," Jason said, as Leo pulled out his gun.

They approached the cabin cautiously and quietly moved to the front door. The door was partially open. The only noise they heard was the wild life in the woods. Leo went first with his gun drawn. He pushed the door open the rest of the way and jumped back. There on the floor was Darcy with a bullet in his head and blood spattered everywhere.

They quickly looked around the one room cabin. Nothing. Jason noticed a cell phone on the floor next to Darcy's body. He picked it up and checked for recent calls. The last two were to Carl Pearlman.

"How well do you know this Pearlman guy?" Jason asked.

"Not well. Like I told you before, when I went to see him, his cronies had me thrown out. After that episode, I did some digging and found out that he was in charge of the Rineheart fortune and Abby's inheritance. That is one of the reasons I went looking for Abby. If this Pearlman guy wouldn't even talk to me, her twin, what would he do to Abby?" Leo replied.

"These last two phone calls were to Pearlman. I think you are right in your assumptions. We better check the shed," Jason said.

He ran out the door toward the shed. His heart was pounding rapidly with fear that they may be too late. The thought of anything happening to Abby was just too hard for him to handle.

When they entered the shed, all they saw were a few tools in the corners. Jason looked down at the dirt floor and saw something silver. He bent down and picked it up.

"This was Abby's."

"Are you sure?"

"I gave it to her when she decided to move in with me. It has a key to my house attached to it. It must have fallen out of her pocket," Jason squeezed it tightly in his fist.

"Jason, look over here by the sickle. Torn duct tape with a little blood on it. Maybe she escaped. In the years I have been following her, she seemed resilient. By the looks of the dirt on the floor, if she was tied, she could have wiggled over and cut the tape with the sickle."

"That means she could be out there somewhere in the woods…in the dark. How do we even begin to find her?"

Jason was heart sick. Just thinking that she could be alone and injured was more than he could bear. He walked out of the shed and looked around. He saw woods in every direction. He just stood there, not knowing what to do next.

"Jason. Come on man, pull it together. I have been following her for years now. I have some idea how she moves. Abby has a natural passion to survive. We just need to take a break here and think it out," Leo said trying to snap Jason out of it. "We can't look for her in the dark. Let's head back to the truck and start out at daybreak."

"She's alone Leo! She could be out there somewhere hurt. I lost one person I loved. I'm not losing another."

"I care about her too! She's my twin. I want a chance to really be with her. Look. We have maybe an hour before we won't be able to see in the front of us. Now, if I was her, I would have wanted to get as far away from the front of the cabin as possible. So, let's try and see if we can pick up any prints in the back of the shed. You did bring a flashlight?" Leo asked.

"Yeah. Okay. Right. Look for prints." It was obvious to Leo that Jason had lost it. He was numb with worry and fear that he lost her.

They went behind the shed. Leo did find prints. One set of small and one set of large boot prints. The prints were not side by side and the large boot prints covered some of the small ones. Almost like they were following them.

"Whoever shot Darcy, could be hunting Abby. Damn it! What do we do?" Jason was at a loss.

"Jason, we have to go back. We will never be able to track her in the dark. I don't want to leave either, but we have to be practical here. Let's get some rest and start out first thing. We won't be doing her any good if we pass out from lack of sleep, and anyhow, I think I'd sense if she wasn't alive."

Jason squeezed the key ring that was in his hand and said, "Yeah. You're right. Let's head back. We'll head to the nearest place from the shed. As soon as there is a shed of light, we haul ass back here."

"Agreed."

Abby jerked awake. She wasn't even sure what woke her. She could see through the gaps in the twigs and leaves, enough to see that it was still night. She silently sobbed. It hit her hard that she had been raped and if she hadn't run, it would have continued until her death. Why did Carl put this on her? If it was her inheritance, damn...she'd just give it to him.

Her thoughts went to Jason. Was he looking for her? How would he ever find her? She missed him, his warm arms, his gentle touch, and the love she saw in his eyes. It made the tears run down her cheeks. If she was to be with him, it would have to be up to her to get out of this and get back to him.

Her thoughts were interrupted by the sound of footsteps breaking twigs and softly crunching leaves. She froze. Her eyes were as big as saucers. She could see a man, with a gun, searching the ground.
He started to mumble to himself, "Where the fuck did she go? Maybe I'll just tell Carl she got away."

She couldn't make out what he looked like, but she knew it wasn't Darcy or Leo. This guy had an Italian accent, and was a lot bigger. He was just about on top of her when she heard a cell phone ring.

"Sully," the man said into the phone in a whisper.

"I lost her," he continued to say. "Her footprints went into the stream. She could have gone in either direction at this point. Carl, man, calm down. She'll show up sooner or later. Maybe that Darcy guy did such a number on her that she bled out. Anyhow, I'm going back to town. Fine, I don't give a fuck. Just pay me for the Darcy kill. I'm out of here for now."

He hung up and turned and headed back the way he came. She let out a breath of air not even realizing she was holding it. Abby's mind was racing in all directions. She could hardly believe that her parents' best friend wanted her dead. All these years that she trusted Carl. No wonder he wanted to know where she was all the time. Then it hit her, Carl wanted her dead before she turned twenty-five, he'd inherit everything. Just what did that all entail? She hadn't a clue, but when she got out of this mess, she intended to find out.

Abby was still afraid to move. She was sore, tired and bloody. She wasn't sure if this Sully was still close by. Lack of food was giving her cramps and a pounding headache. In spite of all that, moving just yet could cost her her life. Maybe she would wait just a while longer.

Sully was back at his vehicle when his cell rang again.

"Sully," was all he said.

"It's me," Carl said, "How about I up the ante?"

"Not now Carl. I'm tired and haven't eaten in a while."

"Listen, you go rest up, then call me back. You can still earn your pay tomorrow. Maybe she will show up somewhere and make your job easier. I just need her dead."

"She could be dead already. Darcy obviously raped her. When I saw her through my goggles, she was all dirty, bloody, and her clothes were torn all up. I heard her screaming before Darcy came out of the shed zipping up his fly," Sully replied. "It's none of my business, but what did this little angel do to you to piss you off so bad?"

"You are right, it is none of your business and "could be's" won't cut it. I need to be sure she is dead. I'll double my offer," Carl said.

"Fine, I'll call you, tomorrow. In the morning, I'll start my search where I left off." Sully hung up, got into his truck and headed back to the nearest town.

Abby awakened to the sound of an owl hooting. It was pitch black. She looked up and saw that the clouds were moving and that the moon was trying to peek through. Not hearing anything, she slowly tried to sit up. Her head pounded and she swayed from dizziness. She felt weak. How would she ever make it to safety? What choice did she have? It was either sit here and die, or find the strength to move. Abby decided to move. Slowly pushing off the ground, she stood. Everything started to spin around her. On her shoulder she felt blood dripping from her head. Darcy had hit her hard with something and split her head open. If she didn't get out of this place, she knew she wouldn't survive.

Abby slowly made her way down to the stream. The cool water felt good on the lump on her forehead. She drank the water from her hands then, again, applied more to her wounds. Looking around as best as she could, she headed up stream away from the cabin. Walking was an extreme effort, but time was of the essence. Who knew how much time she had before some other crony of Carl's came looking for her?

The moon finally came through the clouds and sparkled in the stream. Looking down at herself, she noticed how dirty and tattered her clothes were. She wanted to sleep more, but fear kept her going. Up ahead she saw a farm house. It looked so far away. Her knees could barely hold her up. Coming out of the woods and on to a pasture, her eyes held tightly onto the farm house. She stumbled on a rock and fell down. Lifting her head, all the strength gone, she just laid there and stared at the farm house.

Jason was up before the crack of dawn. So was Leo. They packed up their gear and headed back to the shed where the evidence of Abby's captivity had been. It was just about dawn when they got there.

"Leo, over here. Here are those footprints we saw last night," Jason said while down on his haunches.

Leo knelt down beside him and looked at the prints and the direction they were heading.

"Looks like she headed away from the cabin. Makes sense. Let me check my GPS and see if I get anything."

"Any reception?"

"Nah, not yet. I'll keep trying. Let's follow the tracks and see where it takes us. I have been following Abby for years. She's a survivor," Leo said to Jason, trying to instill some confidence in him.

They were able to follow tracks until they hit a stream. The tracks appeared to head into the water. They stood at the edge of the stream and looked around.

"Now what?" Jason said.

"Hey, look over there. At that ledge. An embankment."

They both walked toward the ledge and found a hole that had been dug out. Leaves were gathered in a pile, and there were traces of blood and long blonde hair attached to them.

"Clever girl! She hid in this hole. I told you she was a survivor. If she made it through the night, she would have gone up stream, away from the cabin. Let's go. I'll check my GPS again," Leo said.

"She's still bleeding. It's killing me to think that she is out there, somewhere, all alone and hurt. We have to find her Leo."

Jason was at wits end.

"I have reception. Not much, but enough to see that there is a farm a few miles ahead. I suggest we head towards it. It's the direction she would have gone. Has to be."

They were sprinting up stream. Sure enough, a few miles ahead, they spotted a farm house in the distance. They broke through the woods and started through the pasture when they spotted a body on the ground.

"Jesus! Abby! Honey! Wake up. Leo, dial 911. Abby honey, I'm here. Wake up."

Jason had fallen to his knees and cradled her body close to his. He checked her neck for a pulse.

"She's alive. Weak, but alive. Sweetheart, I have you. Help is on the way. Hang on baby."

Jason's hands shook as he held her in his arms. He couldn't believe that they had found her.

Abby slowly opened her eyes and looked up at Jason, "You're really here? I'm not dreaming?"

"No baby. You are not dreaming. I have you, and help is on the way," Jason smiled down at her with watery eyes.

"Someone is after me, Jason. We have to get out of here."

"I know sweetheart. You are safe now. Just rest until help arrives. There will be plenty of time to talk later."

Jason held her close to his chest and rocked her slowly.

Leo stayed back so she wouldn't see him. After she received care, he'd have plenty of time to fill her in with everything. Seeing him would just scare her more, thanks to Carl.

"Abby? Honey?" Panic formed in Jason's voice. "Leo, I think she is unconscious. What's the ETA on that ambulance?"

"Maybe ten to fifteen minutes, I'm not sure. Hang in there Jason. She is going to need both of us to keep her safe and get everything under control."

Jason and Leo just stared at her stilled form. Her clothes were dirty, torn and bloody. She had blood in her hair, with a nasty gash on her forehead, and she was extremely pale, but she was alive.

"Carl, I found her. She's not alone," Sully whispered into his cell from behind a large tree.

"Who is she with, and is she still alive?"

"Looks like that Leo guy you had me previously looking for. The other guy, I don't know," Sully relayed while peering through his binoculars. "The other guy is holding her. She ain't movin'. I can't tell if she is dead or not."

"Can't you just kill them all?"

"Are you crazy? You didn't hire me for mass murder. Anyhow, I see an ambulance approaching. Too many witnesses. I'll lay low and check out shit," Sully said, "I'll call you when I have news."

"Stay on it. Get the job done!" Carl yelled then disconnected the call.

Chapter 12

.....................♥ ♥.....................

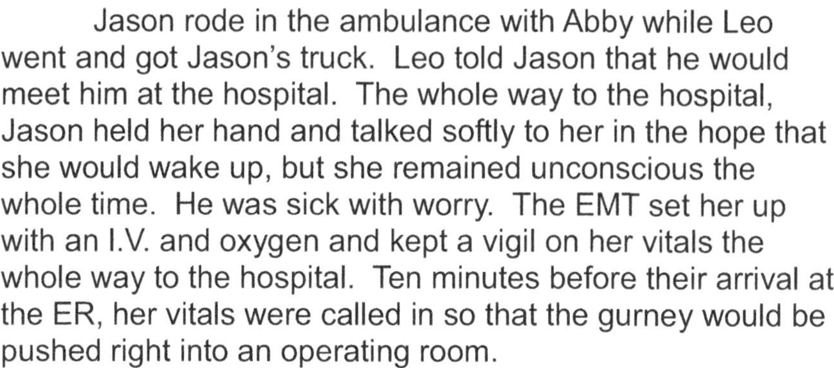

Jason rode in the ambulance with Abby while Leo went and got Jason's truck. Leo told Jason that he would meet him at the hospital. The whole way to the hospital, Jason held her hand and talked softly to her in the hope that she would wake up, but she remained unconscious the whole time. He was sick with worry. The EMT set her up with an I.V. and oxygen and kept a vigil on her vitals the whole way to the hospital. Ten minutes before their arrival at the ER, her vitals were called in so that the gurney would be pushed right into an operating room.

Jason stayed with her until the door closed to the operating room. A nurse stopped him with a gentle hand to his chest and told him to wait there. She would make sure the doctor would come to him as soon as Abby was stable. Jason was standing in the hall when Leo arrived.

"Any news? Did she wake up? Did anyone give you any updates?" Leo was as distraught as Jason.

"No man. Nothing yet. She looked bad Leo. So frail, and still. She has to pull through. I can't imagine going on without her. I should have never left her so soon. If I had stayed home with her, this would have never happened. I can't lose her," Jason was pacing the floor.

"You got to get it together, man," Leo said as he grabbed his arm, "She is going to need both of us steady and strong. This wasn't your fault, so knock this shit off. She has made it this far; she'll make it the rest of the way. I think I would feel it if she wasn't going to make it. Trust me."

"You're right. Thanks Leo," Jason took a deep breath to settle himself.

Just then the doors of the operating room opened and a doctor dressed in scrubs entered the hall.

"Are you the gentleman that arrived with Miss Rineheart?"

"Yes, I'm her boyfriend. She lives with me. Doc, how is she?"

Leo stood beside Jason and said, "I'm her twin. Is she going to be okay?"

"We have her sedated. We need her still. She has some bleeding on the brain, some bruised ribs, and a few broken teeth. She had been raped, so we did a rape kit on her. The police had to be notified. Right now, we have her stabilized. Until we get the bleeding to stop and the swelling to go down, I cannot give a final prognosis. Because she is young and we got things under control, she could come out of this fine. We will know more in a few hours. The sooner she wakes up the better."

"Can we see her?" Jason asked.

"One at a time for now, but yes you can go back with her."

"Thank you doctor," Jason shook his hand.

"I'll keep you informed of her progress. All we can do now is wait," the doctor said, then turned and left.

Jason and Leo just stared at each other, then Leo said, "Jason, you go and stay with her. I can't, not until she knows who I am and that I am not a threat. When the time is right, you can get her up to speed with things. I'll be here, waiting for updates. Go. She is going to need you when she wakes up."

"She will wake up and be fine," Jason said more to himself than to Leo.

He turned and headed into the room where Abby was. When he saw her, he lost control. Tears ran down his cheeks as he slowly approached her bed and gently held her hand. The steady beep of the monitor was the only noise in the room. She looked so still and fragile with a tube stuck into her arm and another tube coming from her nose giving her oxygen. He sat in a chair next to her bed and laid his head down on her stomach, just to have contact with her. He didn't move for hours, and eventually fell asleep holding her hand and listening to her breath.

Outside her door, Leo had to deal with the police when they arrived. He kept everything as vague as possible.

He knew that he and Jason did not want police involved at this point. That could bring Pearlman into the picture, and they had to get things together before that happened. He gave just enough information to keep the police at bay. After they left, he found a couch in the waiting room, closest to Abby's room and eventually fell asleep there.

In the wee hours of the morning, Jason came awake to the slight touch of Abby stroking his hair. He looked up and smiled.

She said, "You look tired sweetheart."

"Baby, you gave me quite a scare. Welcome back. How do you feel?"

"I hurt. Where are we?"

Jason leaned over her and gently kissing her cheek, brushed her hair behind her ear and said, "You are in a hospital in West Virginia. What do you remember, baby?"

Her eyes widened and started to tear up, "Jason, he raped and beat me!"

"I know, baby. I know it was Darcy. There is a lot we have to talk about, but for now, I need you to rest and get stronger, so I can take you home."

"Don't leave me," she said with panic in her voice.

"I'm not going anywhere unless you are right with me. Let me buzz the nurse and see when I can get you out of here. Rest, Abby, you are with me now and I ain't letting you out of my sight. I almost lost you once, that is not happening again," Jason smiled down at her and kissed her cheek again.

The nurse came in and checked Abby's vitals, and let them know that she would notify the doctor. They would have to wait for the doctor to get all their questions answered. While the nurse was with Abby, Jason slipped out the door just long enough to talk to Leo. Leo filled him in on his encounter with the local police.

"Jason, you have to talk to her about me, so we can get her out of here. If she sees me, she will panic. As soon as she is aware of me, let me know so I can see her. I have been going crazy out here wondering how she is," Leo said.

"I know. Just hang in there a while longer. She just woke up. The nurse is with her. We have to wait on the doctor to find out her condition. After I know she is in the clear, I'll fill her in on you. Right now she is pretty shook up. She remembers the rape, Leo. She remembers everything," Jason replied in earnest. "I better get back in there. I don't want her to be alone. I'll come and get you as soon as I know something."

Jason walked back into her room just as the nurse was coming out. He asked if she could have anything to drink or eat, but the nurse said she could only have only ice chips until the doctor gave the okay for something else.

She looked up when he entered, then quickly lowered her head and turned away. The look on her face just about broke Jason's heart in two. She not only looked physically beaten but emotionally, as well. He went to her side and took her hand while he gently kissed her cheek.

"Baby, look at me," he said while lifting her chin with his other hand.

"I can't. I'm afraid."

"You're safe now. What are you afraid of?"

"I'm afraid you won't want me anymore. I feel so dirty. I'm damaged now, Jason."

She looked in his eyes. Her lip trembled, as a tear ran down her cheek Jason already knew that she would think that after what happened to her. If that fucking Darcy wasn't already dead, he would have ripped him to shreds and killed him himself.

"Abby, sweetheart this wasn't your fault. Baby, I could no more turn away from you than breathe without air. If anything, I feel guilty for not staying with you. I could have worked from home. Gave you time to settle in. Believe me, I will never make that mistake again. I thank God that I still have you. You have no idea how crazy I have been knowing that you were gone and I couldn't protect you. Honey, it has shown me one thing for sure……I love you."

Abby reached up slowly and touched his face, "I love you too, Jason."

Jason sat on her bed and lay beside her with his arm

around her, and she nuzzled onto his chest. While lying there, she finally fell back asleep. He just listened to her steady breathing. He wasn't sure how to tell her about Leo, and he wasn't sure how much she knew about what was going on. For now, he just wanted her to rest until the doctor came in.

A few hours later, the doctor came in and was happy with her progress. He wanted to take more x-rays of her head to make sure that the bleeding had indeed stopped. After the x-rays showed that there was no more bleeding, he said that she could leave provided she had total bed rest for two weeks with a follow up with another doctor. He gave her some prescriptions for pain and an antibiotic for possible infection. When the doctor left, Abby sat up and couldn't wait to get out of the hospital.

"Abby, honey, before we leave, we have something we have to talk about, first. We have a lot of things to talk about, but this has to be addressed, first."

Abby looked up at him not sure what to expect.

"You have been misled by that guy named Carl," Jason said.

"I know. Darcy made that perfectly clear."

"Honey, he also lied to you about Leo."

"Leo? The guy who Carl said killed my parents?"

"Baby, he didn't kill your parents. He explained to me in detail and with written legal documentation who he really is, and why he has been following you for so many years. He helped me to find you," Jason said, slowly, as he looked directly into her eyes.

"Who is he then?"

"He's your twin."

Abby took a deep breath and shook her head in disbelief. Jason just gently held her and rocked her slowly, until she settled down a bit.

"Honey, it is the truth. I had his background checked, and his documents appear to be legitimate. He is your twin. He has been outside in the hall this whole time waiting for me to tell you about him, so he could come and talk to you himself. There is so much that you need to know and understand. But for now, just let him talk to you. I know you will feel better about it all if you just face him."

"Don't leave me alone with him," Abby said with fear in her eyes.

"I told you already that I am not leaving your side. I'll be here the whole time. Are you ready?"

"I'm scared, but, okay."

Jason got up and left the room for no more than a couple minutes, then appeared again with Leo right behind him. The shock of seeing Leo up close made Abby shake all over. Jason immediately lay beside her in the hospital bed and held her close to him. Leo slowly walked over to the side of her bed and took her hand.

"Abby, I have waited for years for this moment. I am your twin brother and I did not kill our parents. Look at my face. Look in my eyes. I know you know me."

Leo looked her in the eye and just waited while she took it all in.

It was like she was hit with an awareness. At first she just stared at him. Then she slowly smiled. She squeezed his hand and stared into his eyes and knew instantly who he was. Tears started to roll down her cheeks as she smiled up at him.

"I know who you are," was all she said.

She reached up for him to hug her. He watered up, smiled and hugged her gently.

"We have a lot of catching up to do, sis. Let's get you out of here and back to Jason's house, first," Leo said softly while taking his fingers and pushing a strand of her hair off her cheek and gently curling it behind her ear.

Chapter 13

The ride back to Jason's house was spent filling each other in with all that had transpired before Abby and Leo's parents died. Abby would still be convalescing for at least two more weeks (if Jason and Leo had their way, it would be a lot longer!).

Jason was amazed at how Abby and Leo really did resemble each other. They had the same eye and hair color. He was also surprised at how quickly they reconnected. He figured that that was what Leo was counting on. That she would sense the connection just as Leo had. Once Abby saw Leo up close and held his hand, Jason saw the instant recognition in her eyes when she looked up at Leo.

Jason's house was certainly big enough, so he told Leo to stay with them as long as he wanted. He was family. Anyway, there was business to iron out, like tending to Carl.

Abby was set up in her own bedroom, for the time being. Jason didn't want to disturb her while she convalesced. With all the drugs she was given, she slept a lot. He still had to contend with his work, which he directed from home. There was no way he was going to let her out of his sight for any length of time. Jason knew that Dave could take care of the crew and the work site. Dave worked with his dad for a long time before Jason took over. If there were any problems only the owner could resolve, Jason would try to deal with them from home.

Leo and Jason took turns looking in on Abby around the clock, although Jason spent the majority of the time with her. Leo would relieve him only so he could catch a few hours' sleep.

Abby was sleeping soundly. It was early evening. Jason and Leo were in the living room, sitting in front of the fireplace watching a football game on the big screen.

"Any ideas on how to proceed with any of this?" Jason asked.

"Maybe Abby will remember something that can help us figure out which direction to go. It hasn't even been a full week yet, though, so I hate to even bring anything up to her. What do you think?" Leo asked as he turned and faced Jason.

"She still hasn't slept through the night without jumping up fully awake. I don't know, Leo. That Darcy guy really fucked her up. She may be healing physically but mentally and emotionally is going to take a while."

They both jumped up as they heard a blood curdling scream coming from Abby. They ran up the steps, three at a time, barged into her room and flicked on the lights. Abby was sitting up in bed, shaking like a leaf, eyes big as saucers, and covered in sweat. Jason ran to one side and Leo ran to the other.

"Sweetheart, you're o.k. You had another nightmare. We are right here. No one can get you," Leo said as he climbed in bed beside her.

Jason was already beside her and hugging her close to him, while rubbing soothing strokes up and down her back. He looked over her head at Leo and saw the worried look on his face. Jason felt the same way.

"Baby, talk to us. Maybe if you tell us what you saw, it will help," Jason whispered in her ear.

"I'm not safe," she said, "He's still coming for me. He said he would." She looked at both of them with tears running down her cheeks. "He's not going to give up until I'm dead."

"Who's coming for you, Abby?" Leo asked.

"Sully."

Jason and Leo gave each other a puzzled look. Jason asked, "Who is Sully?"

"When I ran from the shed, into the woods, I ran until I came to a stream. It was getting dark, and I was so tired, and my head hurt. I knew I had to find shelter before I fell over. I dug a hole in the bank of the stream and buried myself in leaves and twigs. I fell asleep for a while and then woke up to a noise," she said as she looked at both of them.

Leo got up to get her a drink of water, while Jason held on to her and asked her, "What did you hear?"

"I heard twigs breaking. I could see a figure through the leaves that were covering me. I was so scared that I froze completely still. He was a big man. I never saw him before. He was mumbling to himself saying that he was wondering where I went. Then I heard a cell phone ringing."

Leo handed her the water with one of her pain pills, and she drank the whole glass.

"Go on, sweetheart. We are right here listening," Leo said.

"He answered it saying his name was Sully. Then he said Carl's name. He was talking to Carl! How could Carl do this to me? He was daddy's best friend. How?" She started to cry again.

"Take it easy, honey. We will figure this out. We won't leave your side until we do," Leo answered.

Jason held her and rocked her until she went back to sleep. Lying there with her, he watched her as she gently breathed, and he looked at her tear stained face. It tore him up that she was hurting so badly; he thought his heart would break. Leo motioned from the door for Jason to join him. He hated to leave her for even a minute, but he knew that if they were going to figure this out, they had to put their heads together. He gently slid away from her and laid her head on the pillow. He kissed her forehead, and tucked her in with the blankets. She didn't even stir.

As soon as they got to the living room, Leo said, "I knew that Carl was crooked. That Sully guy must be a hit man for hire. You have anybody that can do some digging?"

"As a matter of fact, I have a few "ins" with the police department here. It's time I collect on some past due favors. Meanwhile, didn't you mention that you have done some investigating of your own? I have a computer, maybe you can see what you can find out about this Carl guy," Jason replied.

"I'm on it, just lead the way to your computer."

Chapter 14

Carl hadn't heard from Sully for several days, and he was getting impatient. He decided it was time to find out if he had made any progress. He dialed Sully's cell and waited as it rang.

"Sully here."

"Why haven't you called? Have you completed the job? What's going on, and where the hell are you?"

"Easy, Carl. Do you want the job done right? That takes planning. I have followed her from the hospital to this guy's house, a Jason Donahue. You know him?"

"No. I have no idea who he is. What have you found out?" Carl asked.

"It appears that this Donahue guy owns a construction company that your Darcy got a job at. Sound familiar now?"

"Darcy never mentioned what he was doing on the job. Anyhow, what does that have to do with Abby?"

"Well, he not only owns a construction company but also a huge house that has a state of the art security system. Inside is your Abby AND Leo."

"Fuck! How do you know this? Have you seen them?" Carl asked.

"I followed all three of them home from the hospital. Donahue carried her in and Leo followed close behind. I'm able to view inside the large living room window and from what I've seen, Donahue and Leo have been hanging out together talking. They must have put her in another room to heal. Like I said, Darcy did a number on her."

"That means that she and Leo know each other. Shit! They know about me. This is getting out of hand. You have to kill them. I don't care how you do it. Blow the whole fucking house down. I need them dead!" Carl screamed into the phone.

"Take it easy Carl. It has only been a couple days.

Let me do some surveillance and see if I can flush them out. No sense in taking unnecessary risks and drawing attention to myself. That's not how I operate. If you don't like how I am handling things, you can always hire someone else and just pay me for the Darcy kill. It's up to you," Sully said with confidence.

"No. Just get it done. Keep me posted and hurry. Call me when you have any new information," Carl said in a very irritated voice and then hung up.

"Well, good-bye to you too asshole," Sully barked into his disconnected cell.

Usually, Sully didn't mind doing a job, but he had trouble with watching innocent women or children being hurt. He was almost ready to walk away from this one. If he hadn't witnessed Abby getting beat up and raped, maybe it would have been a little easier. This just had wrong written all over it. He was going to give it a couple more days to see what happened. See if there were any habits - of any of them leaving the house. If things didn't clean up, he was just going to walk away.

Sully started to set up various sites around the house, trying to gain access to a clear view in the upstairs windows. He could follow the three of them by their heat signatures, but Leo and Jason were pretty much the same size with Jason being a few inches taller. Abby seemed to be stationary in an upstairs bedroom. No clear looks in that bedroom anyhow. He figured that she was still pretty much drugged by the lack of movement. Healing takes time. A couple more days should show some movement. That gave him time to stabilize the sites, so he could get a clear look without being detected. The wooded area in the back of the house allowed for many such sites in the trees.

Jason headed into the kitchen to find Leo getting a beer. "Hey man," Jason said, "it is getting late. I'm heading to bed after I check on Abby. We can start again, tomorrow. Why don't you get some shut eye?"

"I'm good. I just want to check a few things out then I'm heading up also. See ya in the morning. And,

Jason, thanks for letting me stay here. I am really looking forward to spending time with my sister. We have a lot of catching up to do."

"You are welcome to stay as long as you like. You are family. Anyhow, we have our work cut out for us if we want to get to the bottom of all the shit that has happened. Maybe tomorrow, Abby will be more alert and can fill us in with all that had happened to her. We need to get some info on Carl."

"Yeah that's for sure. Well, goodnight."

"Goodnight, Leo,"

With that Jason headed up the steps to check on Abby. When he got to her room, he gently opened the door and quietly walked in. He checked to see her chest rise to make sure she was breathing. So badly he wanted to climb in with her and hold her, but he was afraid that her body was still too sore from all the bruises.

He stood by her bed and lightly kissed her forehead and softly said, "I love you sweetheart. Have good dreams." He backed out quietly and shut her door. He missed her so badly and wanted her back in his bed where she belonged. That would have to wait until she was better. Opening his bedroom door, he took off his clothes and climbed into bed without even turning on his light. The strain of all that had happened in the past few days finally hit him. He fell asleep as soon as his head hit the pillow.

Chapter 15

.......................♥ ♥......................

Abby suddenly jumped up sitting in bed. It was still dark. The clock on the nightstand said 3 a.m. She shook all over and was covered in sweat. Looking around, she remembered that she was in Jason's house in her bedroom, and she was afraid. Her heart was beating hard and she was gasping for air. "I don't want to be alone," she whispered to herself. Slowly she climbed out of bed and headed to Jason's bedroom. Ever so gently, she crept into his room and slowly climbed into his bed. Jason didn't stir. She curled up against him and went back to sleep.

Jason heard her the moment she opened his door, but he didn't want to frighten her. It warmed his heart that she wanted to be close to him to feel safe. He hoped she would spend all her nights right there beside him. He slowly turned, as not to wake her, and placed her back against his chest, and snuggled her close with his arm around her waist. She whimpered a bit but then settled back into a deep sleep. Just having her there, knowing she was alive and that he didn't lose her, was more than enough for now.

The morning light started to shine in Jason's bedroom window.

"Waking up to a soft Abby tucked next to me is the only way to start the day," Jason thought to himself. Having her sweet ass cheeks pressed up against his dick woke it up too. He knew that he was just going to have to ignore it. Abby began to wake up. He brushed her hair off her face and gave her a gentle kiss on her forehead. "Good morning, sunshine. How are you feeling?"

"I hope you aren't mad at me for climbing in your bed. I had a nightmare and was scared," she said without moving.

"Honey, you are right where you belong. Here with me. I would have brought you here as soon as we came back from the hospital, but you were pretty bruised and drugged up, and I didn't want to hurt you. I loved that you came to me."

"Feels like someone else is glad I climbed in also."

"Just ignore it. It can't be helped. He has a mind of his own, and he misses you so much. Having your ass cheeks rubbed up against him has him in a tizzy," Jason said with a boyish grin.

Abby turned to face him. She placed her hand on his face, looked into his eyes, and slowly eased into him and kissed him. Jason pulled her towards him and pushed her mouth open ever so gently and with his tongue took control of the kiss. She gave a slight moan and wrapped her arm around his back. She reached down to caress his ass cheek with a firm squeeze. He pulled back and looked into her eyes.

"Abby, are you sure about this. I can wait. You are still bruised. I don't want to hurt you."

"I have missed you too," she replied with glassy eyes. "I want to erase all those bad nightmares. I can't see a better way than making love with you."

"Here baby, why don't you get on top, that way you can control how much you can take. We will take it slow."

Jason grabbed her waist and helped her to straddle him. Once she was there, he rested his hands on her thighs and looked up at her, "Tell me what you want Abby. Let me help you make it good."

"Touch me," she leaned over his chest, "put your mouth on my nipples and suck me."

With a whimper he leaned up and suckled, first one breast, then the other. Each time he sucked the sensation shot straight to her clit. Abby gasped. It seemed like it had been forever since he felt her and it made his eyes roll back in his head. His hands automatically reached up to caress her ass. She could feel his cock straining against her belly. She felt herself getting wet, her body getting ready for him. All she wanted was to feel his cock inside her. Leaning back up, their eyes met, and she saw nothing but love and desire in him. She reached down and grabbed his penis; he hissed taking in air through gritted teeth. Looking down she started to lower but couldn't. Darcy popped into her head. Instead, she looked back into Jason's eyes while she rubbed up and down his shaft with her hand feeling him swell more. Jason just smiled and said, "Baby, just do what makes you feel comfortable. You are the one controlling this. I won't get angry, I understand. Do you want to stop?"

"No. I just....I want you Jason."

He reached up with both hands to cup her head, "You already have me sweetheart," he softly whispered to her. As turned on as he was, he knew she had to work past the demons that were scaring her. "Take what you need, I can wait."

She rose onto her knees, and guided the tip of his cock into her wet pussy. She slowly lowered herself onto him, feeling it filling her up. Looking at his face, she could see the muscles in his jaw clench as he fought to maintain control. After he was fully seated in her, she tilted her head back with her eyes closed and sighed.

"Abby, honey, look at me." She looked down at him. "It's me, Jason. It's me you are making love with."

She slowly smiled, teared up and said, "I know."

She started to move up and down, and Jason helped her with his hands under her ass. She could feel him throbbing inside of her, and her body responded by gripping him tighter. She could feel every vain in his shaft. He let out a groan while gritting his teeth. She put her hands on his chest for support. Her long blonde curls cascaded around her. She started speeding up the motion.

"Baby, it has been awhile. Being inside you ....I'm so close to coming," Jason said in between gasps of breath.

"I'm ready, Jason. Take me. You take me."

He grabbed her to his chest and rolled them over so he was on top. He looked into her eyes and saw desire not fear. He kissed her while tonguing her mouth and began fucking her. He could feel her heart beating as fast as his. He slowly glided his cock out until the head of it was just touching her folds. Then he thrust back in and filled her to the hilt, repeating over and over. All that could be heard was

skin against skin as his balls hit her ass cheeks. With one hand he reached down and rubbed her clit. That was all it took to put her over the edge as she cried out his name. He kissed her screams and gave one hard thrust.
"Aaah...Abby, I'm coming. You feel so fucking tight and I can't hold on anymore". He thrust hard and fast and shot his cum inside her. "Fuck....." Jason shouted as spurt after spurt came with each thrust.

They both collapsed and he quickly supported himself up on his forearms so as not to crush her. He gently kissed her and rolled to her side, lying on his side facing her.

"Did I hurt you?" Jason asked while trying to catch his breath.

"No. I needed this as much as you did. I needed to feel totally connected to you again."

"Do you want to talk about it?" Jason asked while brushing her hair out of her eyes.

"I know I have to talk to both you and Leo. Can we shower and eat first? I think we both worked up a good sweat. I want to get up and move around. "

"Sounds like a good idea. I don't want you leaving the house unless I or Leo are with you, though. It isn't safe outside yet," Jason said.
He watched her as she got up out of bed and saw her wince.

"Ahh.., Sweetheart, you are still sore. Here let me help you get into the shower. Maybe the hot water will help."

He came around the bed. He lifted her into his arms and carried her to the bathroom. He sat her down gently on the bath counter, and started the water. When it was hot enough, he lifted her up and stood her under the spray, then climbed in behind her. She winced and groaned as the water sprayed down on her.

This was the first time he had seen her fully naked since she had been kidnapped and it made his heart and chest clench at the black and blue marks all over her body. That bastard really fucked her up.

He lathered a sponge and gently soaped her all over, then himself. He rinsed them both. He shampooed and rinsed her hair. She didn't say a word and looked completely drained. Turning off the water he reached for a towel and dried off quickly, then got another towel and lifted her out and dried her. After drying her hair, he ran a brush through it. He then wrapped her up in his robe and wrapped a towel around himself. He picked her up and walked her to her room.

"Abby, I'm going to go start breakfast. Take your time. When you are ready to come downstairs, call out. You look too weak, and I don't want you walking down the steps yet. Leo or I will come and get you." He kissed her forehead and said, "I love you."

"I love you," she answered with a weak smile.

He slowly closed her door, and went to get dressed. He was hoping that Leo was up, so they could discuss their next move before Abby joined them. Seeing all the bruises all over her body broke his heart. No one will ever get to her again, as long as he was alive. He swore this to God. He saw how she hesitated while sitting on top of him. He could see the fear in her eyes in the beginning. He knew it would take time before she felt safe again, and he knew that until they got this Carl guy, neither Abby nor Leo would be safe. Walking downstairs he listened at her door and heard her moving around, so he headed for the kitchen.

Leo was already there brewing coffee. He turned and looked at Jason, "How's Abby?"

"Man, that fucker did a real number on her. It's going to take a lot of time for her to get over this. She had another nightmare, and snuck into my room about 3 in the morning. She climbed in my bed, wet with sweat and shaking like a leaf. She will be in with me from now on."

"That's good. She'll do better being with you. Hey, I did some research," Leo said, and handed Jason some printouts of what he found.

Jason started reading when they both heard Abby call out, "I'll get her. Can you cook?"

"I can make bacon and eggs," Leo said.

"Good enough. Get it going. After we eat, Abby wants to talk to both of us. She said there are some things she has to discuss with both of us. Here, keep these print outs handy. We'll need to go over them also."

"God love her," Jason thought. She was waiting at the top of the steps leaning against the wall. With her big green eyes and long blonde hair, she looked like a delicate waif. He ran up the steps and picked her up like she weighed nothing. He carried her to the kitchen. Before he set her down on a stool by the kitchen table, she reached up and hugged his neck and kissed him firmly on the lips.

"What was that for?" he asked with a smile.

"Just had to do it," she said, and smiled back.

"Feel free to do that all the time," he said, as he placed her on a stool.

"Hey, Sis," Leo said. "How'd ya sleep?" he said with a wink.

She blushed, "Oh, just fine."

After they all ate, Jason started reading the printouts. Afterward he looked up at Leo, "Where did you find this shit out?"

"I have my ways," Leo said, looking serious.

"What's going on?" Abby asked.

"Did you know that Carl has control of mom and dad's estate?" Leo asked Abby.

"Yes. He would send me money whenever I had to move, or for my expenses."

"Did you know that that control stops on your 25th birthday, and that you have full control unless you should die before hand?" Leo looked directly at her but asked gently.

"I wasn't sure about that, but I knew that the account that is in my name would become mine solely at 25."

"No honey. It ALL becomes yours at 25," Jason said as he was reading the information in front of him.

"What's all?"

"Over 1.2 billion plus real estate," Leo answered.

Abby just stared at both of them feeling woozy. She started to sway, and they both jumped up to catch her. Jason picked her up, carried her to the living room, and sat her on the couch. Jason sat beside her and Leo sat in front of her.

"I knew mom and dad were rich. I just didn't know

how rich. This explains why Carl wants us dead. Before I managed to escape from Darcy, he told me that it was him that cut dad's car brakes. Leo, he told me that Carl hired him to kill them both. Darcy must have found out about their money, because he kept calling me "rich little chicky"."

"Did Carl ever show any signs after their death?"

"No. That's just it. He treated me like he really cared about me. I hadn't a clue that he hated our parents. All these years he acted like I meant something to him," Abby said in a daze. Her eyes watered as she looked at both of them. "How could I not sense something was wrong?"

"Honey, don't blame yourself," Jason said, "You are not responsible for his actions. What I want to know is who killed Darcy?"

"Sully," Abby said. "When I was holed up in the embankment at the stream, I heard Sully say to Carl that he shot Darcy."

"So Sully is a hired gun, just as I thought," Leo said, "Honey, did you happen to get a look at him?"

"Yeah. He was tall with broad shoulders, with dark hair and eyes. He had an Italian accent."

"Abby, you look whipped. Let's go out on the porch. You can sit with me on the swing and take a little break. Leo, can you do some more of your magic, and snoop around, and see what you can find?"

"Right on it. You two go be a normal couple for a bit and swing away," Leo said with a grin.

Chapter 16

It was still late morning. The air was fresh and warm. Jason's porch swing was large enough for three. It had a cushy pad, making it very relaxing. Jason had his arm around Abby's shoulders. He was watching her as she was taking in the view.

"What are you looking at, sweetheart? " Jason asked. He saw her leaning over and straining to see in the woods.

"What's that shiny thing over there in the trees?"

Jason looked up in the direction she was pointing. He quickly grabbed her and they both fell to the floor as a shot pinged just above them.

"What the fuck was that?" Leo shouted as he held open the screen door.

"Get back inside Leo! Somebody's in the woods and just took a shot at Abby!" Jason yelled.

Just then another shot went through the screen door and Leo hit the floor. Abby screamed. Jason grabbed her and rolled her with him under the swing to the side of the porch. He then picked her up in his arms and ran to the back of the house. Going in the back door, he ran to the kitchen and placed Abby on a chair and said, "Stay right here. Don't go by any windows. Here's my phone, dial 911. I'm checking on Leo."

Jason ran to the living room. He saw Leo on the floor in a pool of blood. He bent down feeling for a pulse and found one. It was weak but there. Leo was out cold. Jason pulled off his tee shirt and applied pressure to Leo's shoulder where the bullet hit. Abby came in. She saw Leo and gasped.

"He's alive Abby," Jason said, "It's deep, but he'll make it."

"There is so much blood," Abby said, then sobbed.

"Honey, I need you to hold it together until the

ambulance gets here," Jason told her and motioned her to come beside him. He didn't want her standing in case the shooter was still nearby. "Can you hold this shirt and apply pressure?" He figured it would help her to focus.

"Yeah, I can do that. The ambulance said they would be here in five minutes," Abby said. She stopped crying as soon as she felt she was helping her brother.

A few minutes went by before they could hear the siren. A couple minutes more and the EMTs had a gurney in Jason's living room and were tending to Leo. The Sheriff came in behind the medics.

Sheriff Cooper stood about six feet tall and had a slight gut. A good man, although he had seen better days. He was graying around the edges, but still a damn good sheriff. The town knew and loved him. He had known Jason since birth. In fact, he bowled on Thursdays with Jason's dad.

"Jason, what kind of trouble did you get yourself into now," Sheriff Cooper said, as he shook Jason's hand.

"Hey Coop, it's a long story, and I'm going to need your help. Can we talk at the hospital? This is Abby, my fiancée. And this is her twin brother, and we need to get him moving," Jason said.

Abby was so busy attending to Leo, it didn't even register with her what Jason had said. He was glad too, because this was not the way he had planned to propose to her. He said it so Coop would understand just how important she was to him.

"I want to ride with Leo," Abby said.

"Jason, ride with me. We can get there faster with a police escort," Sheriff Cooper said.

Jason covered Abby with a huge hooded coat, just in case the shooter was still around. He walked her to the ambulance. He then climbed into the sheriff's car and they were off.

"Carl, this is Sully. I shot them both but I'm not sure of the outcome. An ambulance and police car just left heading for the hospital," Sully said.

“What do you mean by you’re not sure of the outcome? Did you kill them or not?” Carl was obviously frustrated.

“I’m pretty sure Leo is dead, but Abby had to be carried into the house. I’m going to scout the hospital and see what I got. I’ll call you when I know something,” Sully hung up. He wasn’t in the mood for Carl’s bullshit.

On the way to the hospital, Jason filled in Sheriff Cooper with all the details. By the time they reached the hospital, Coop was on board and willing to help in any way he could. He knew that Jason was an honest and good man. He was proud of the work that Jason did in the military. He immediately sent some men out to search Jason’s property to see if they could find any clues that could bring them closer to the shooter.

Jason sat in the waiting room, holding Abby in his lap. It had been several hours by then, and Leo was still in the operating room. Suddenly, a doctor came through the double doors and went to the sheriff. The sheriff led the doctor straight to Jason and Abby. They both stood.

“We were able to remove the bullet that was lodged into his shoulder blade. He has lost a lot of blood,” the doctor said.

“Is he going to be okay?” Abby asked fearfully.

“He may not have use of his one arm, but the main problem is he has a rare blood type, AB negative, and we don’t have any in stock. Without a transfusion, he could die.”

“Take my blood,” Abby said without hesitation.

“Do you know your blood type,” the doctor asked.

“It has to be the same as his, we are twins,” Abby said.

“Come with me. We’ll do a quick check first while we are suiting you up for the transfusion.”

Jason gave her a firm hug, kissed her forehead and said, “I’ll be right here waiting for you.”

Sheriff Cooper sat with Jason in the waiting room. There were only two other people there when they arrived, a couple asleep in the corner. Jason lost all concept of time.

Worry had consumed him. Before Sheriff Cooper went to get them both a cup of coffee, he asked Jason, “Do your folks know about any of this? Are they aware of Abby?”

“I was planning on taking her over to them once she had time to heal, but now this happened.”

“I’m supposed to meet your dad later. You want me to fill them in?” Coop asked.

“No. I want to be the one to tell them. I don’t know how long I’ll be here, so I’ll just call them while I’m waiting.”

While the sheriff was gone, a strange man walked in. He stared straight at Jason and said, “Hey man. What’s up? My wife is having a baby. Is that what you are here for? Your wife delivering, too?”

Jason just stared at him like the guy was a little nuts, but then he did notice the accent. It was Italian. “No. Are you from around here?”

“No,” the man said, “but my wife wanted to come to this hospital. Women, ya know?”

“Yeah,” Jason replied. He wanted to keep him talking until Coop came back, in the hope that Coop might know him.

“Hey, I hear that there was a shooting around here. Are you here because of that?”

Just then Coop came through the door with two coffees in his hand. The man stood up and said, “Well, I best get back. Good luck to you.” He couldn’t leave quickly enough.

“Coop, did you know that guy?”

“No, why?”

“He was acting funny and asking stupid questions,” Jason said.

“We do have a few stupid people around here you know.”

“With an Italian accent?” Jason said seriously.

While Sheriff Cooper went to look for the man, Jason looked up and saw the doctor coming through the doors. Jason stood and went over to him.

"Doctor, how are they?"

"Abby's blood pressure is a little low. I understand you are Abby's fiancé'. Are you aware of the bruises all over her body, and it appears she had head trauma?" the doctor asked.

"Yes. She was the one that was kidnapped and raped. Her brother and I found her in a field and called 911," Jason answered.

"I do recall hearing about that. Normally we wouldn't allow this because of her low blood pressure, but she is insisting. Are you willing to co-sign for her?"

"Is she in any danger?"

"There is always a danger when dealing with this type of procedure. I think it will be minimal, but hospital policy requires a second signature due to her condition," the doctor said.

"Can I see her first?"

"Sure, follow me."

The doctor led him directly to Abby and then said, "Make this quick. We don't have a lot of time here if you want to save her brother."

"Baby," Jason said as he grabbed Abby's hand, "are you sure about this? The doctor is worried about you, and so am I."

"Jason, please just sign. I'll be okay. They said I'll be a little weak for a while, but that's all. If I don't do this, I could lose my twin before I ever get to really know him," Abby pleaded.

"Okay honey. I love you. I'll sign, but before I do there is something I need to ask you."

She looked up at him and asked, "What?"

"Will you marry me?" Jason was shaking all over.

Abby gasped. Her eyes opened wide and started to water, "Yes," was all she could say, then she reached to hug him.

Jason left out a breath, not even realizing that he was holding it. He smiled and said, "Now you have to be okay. You have a wedding to plan. I love you so much, Abby."

"I love you too. You'll see, I'll be fine. I have too

much to live for."

"Go save your brother," Jason said, as he left the room.

After signing the paperwork, Jason headed back to the waiting room to find the sheriff waiting on him.

"Did you find that guy?" Jason asked.

"No. He beat it out of here like a bat out of hell. My deputy noticed him rushing out and got a partial plate, make and model of vehicle. We are running it now. How's your girl and her brother doing?"

"I don't know yet, Coop. Abby is still weak from her ordeal, so I had to sign additional papers to release the hospital to take her blood. Leo is still out of it. I could lose both of them."

"Don't think like that. They are both young. They will both pull through," Coop said to him.

"I've lost one fiancée, I don't think I could handle losing another," Jason replied.

"Why don't you call your folks? I'm sure that they would want to be here with you. I'm going to head back to the station and see what I can find out about all of this. Don't worry, you'll be the first to know if I do. Hang in there Jason," he said.

Coop gave him a hug and pat on the back, then left.

It was quiet in the waiting room. Jason was the only one there at that moment. His chest was tight with fear and worry. He really didn't know if he could stand to lose Abby. He knew from the first time he saw her that she belonged to him. He never thought it could happen again for him, but it did. Every time he saw her, his heart would skip a beat. Her smile could wipe away a rotten day. Those lunchtimes were the most important times. The mornings would drag until he would see her leaving her apartment with those two glasses of iced tea.

He thought to himself, "Maybe I should call mom and dad, because if something bad does happen….." He dialed his parents' phone number, "Mom? It's Jas. I need to talk to you and dad. Do you think you guys could come down to the hospital waiting room?"

"Jason, sweetheart, are you okay?" his mother said. He could hear the panic in her voice.

"I'm not hurt, mom, but I could really use you and dad's support. I'll explain everything when you get here."

"We'll be right there, son," she said, then quickly hung up.

It only took his parents about twenty minutes to get there. They both rushed in and hugged him. His dad spoke first.

"What's going on, son? Why are you here?"

"Mom and dad, come over here and sit down with me. I have a lot to fill you in on," Jason said, as he led them to the corner of the room.

He started to fill them in from the very beginning, his lunch times with a beautiful girl.

"You've met someone?" his mom asked.

"Why didn't you bring her over to meet us?" his dad asked.

"I was planning to, but things got sidetracked," Jason answered.

"What happened? Is she the one in the other room that you are here waiting for?" his mom asked.

"Yes. I'm not sure she is going to be alright. If she isn't, I don't know if I could stand it because, mom and dad, I asked her to marry me and she said yes," Jason said, and his eyes watered up.

His mom started crying as she hugged her son. His dad said softly, "Tell us what happened, son."

Jason explained how he met her at the apartment complex where he had been working for months, and that they met and talked every day. They didn't start to get real serious until a couple months ago, and then she was kidnapped.

Just then, his mother's cell phone went off. "Hello," she said, "I'm over at the hospital. No, it's not me. It has to do with your brother. Why don't you just come here, I think he could use us all here. We'll explain when you get here. See you soon, honey."

"That was Debbie. She is on her way," his mom said.

"Good. I really didn't want to introduce her to you all this way, but if she gets through this, I want her to know that she has family," Jason said.

"What do you mean, if? She sounds like a pretty tough cookie. She'll make it," his father said.

Jason continued to fill them in on Leo and how he helped to find Abby.

"I would have never found her without him," Jason commented.

Just then Debbie entered. She went straight to Jason and hugged him firmly.

"What's going on big brother?" Debbie asked with love and concern in her eyes.

"Your brother's fiancée is in the operating room with her twin, who is laying on death's bed. She is giving blood in hopes to save him," Jason's dad said, trying to catch her up to where they were.

"You're getting married? When were you going to let me in on this?" Debbie asked.

"Sis, I was just explaining all of this before you arrived. Mom and dad can fill you in," Jason said as he rose up to meet the doctor at the door.

"Doc, how's Abby?" Jason asked.

"We were able to stabilize her. She's quite weak from donating blood, but she will be fine with plenty of rest. You can go see her if you want, she is asking for you," the doctor said.

"How's Leo?"

"She saved his life. He is resting comfortably also," the doctor said with a smile, and headed back through the double doors.

Jason just stood there with tears running down his cheeks. He didn't even know he was crying, the relief was so great. He turned and looked at his family. They were standing close and looking at him.

"Could you please stay until I come back? I have to go hug my girl," he said with a smile.

"We'll all be right here, son," his father said, "You go

and then let us know when we can meet the newest member of the family. Meanwhile, we will fill your sister in on what has all transpired."

Jason turned and followed the doctor. When he entered the room, she was on her side sleeping. He could hear the beeping of the heart monitor with its steady beat. She had an I.V. connected to her left wrist giving her fluids and a tube in her nose giving her oxygen. She looked so tiny and frail curled up in the bed that it made his heart twist. Oh how he loved this woman. He slowly walked over to her and took her hand. When he did, she woke up and smiled.

"I did it. I told you I could," she said.

"Yes you did, sweetheart," he said.

"The doctor told me that Leo will be alright, and after we rest a bit, we can all go home," she said.

"Yes we can. The sooner the better," he said as he kissed her forehead, "My future wife has a wedding to plan."

"Yes I do, and I can't wait."

"Honey, your future family is outside wanting to meet you when you are ready," Jason said softly.

"All of them? How?" she looked overwhelmed.

"I called my parents. I wanted them to know about you. As soon as I called and told them I was here, they all came. I told them about what has happened and they stayed to help keep me calm. They are eager to meet you, but if it is too much, it can wait until another time."

"If they came with just a phone call, they must really love you. I never had that before. If you think they will accept me then, yeah, I'd love to meet them," she said.

"I have no doubt that they will love you," Jason replied, "I'll go get them."

Jason stepped back into the waiting room and motioned them to come in. The three of them slowly entered, so as to not make too much noise. They didn't want to alarm her. As soon as they saw her, they all smiled. Jason's mom went over to her and gave her a warm hug,

"We are all so very glad to meet you, Abby. We won't stay too long, but as soon as you are stronger, we do expect you to be at Sunday dinner. You get better now."

"Jason was planning on bringing me a while ago, until all this happened," Abby said, "I'm looking forward to it."

"I have a new sister!" Debbie said.

She came around the other side of the bed and also gave her a hug.

"We have to get together soon, so I can fill you in on my brother's shenanigans"

"Jason told me all about you. I'm looking forward to doing girl things with you," Abby said in a weak voice. She was fighting to keep her eyes open, and Jason noticed.

"Come on everybody. She needs her rest. I'll bring her to mom's as soon as she is stronger," Jason said as he herded everyone to the door.

"You be sure to bring your brother with you young lady," his dad said as he planted a kiss on her forehead.

She smiled up at him and slowly nodded her head.

Jason walked everyone into the waiting room and promised he would call as soon as he had her home. Right then, all he wanted was to be with her. They all understood and after kisses and hugs, they parted ways.

When Jason walked back into her room, she was sound asleep. He decided to check on Leo who was just a couple rooms away. When he walked in he saw the same man who had been asking him questions in the waiting room. The stranger had a hypodermic needle in his hand and was sticking it into Leo's I.V. while he was sleeping. Jason charged the guy with a fist to the face, hearing bones crunch, he knew he broke the guy's nose. Blood spurted everywhere. The man fell back hitting a tray, knocking it over, making a loud noise that echoed into the hallway. The guy gained his balance to swing back, aiming for Jason's stomach, but Jason was too quick and he missed. Jason then chopped his jugular with the side of his hand and the man went down with a thud. By then security was called. They ran in grabbing the stranger who was face down on the floor, and they handcuffed him. They had to lift him to carry him out into the hall

"Somebody get in here. I don't know if that guy poisoned Leo or not," Jason yelled into the hall. "Leo, wake up man! Don't you dare die on us, now!" Jason said while leaning over his bed.

The nurse ran in and found the needle on the floor. It was still full. She checked Leo's vitals. He was fine, just still in a deep sleep from the medication. She had the doctor paged to be sure of her findings.

Jason went into the hall and caught up with security. He stood in front of the stranger and yelled, "Are you Sully?"

"Who wants to know?" the man answered.

Just then, Sheriff Cooper came down the hall and said to Jason, "Yeah, that's him and he is under arrest for attempted murder."

"And murder, Coop. He killed the guy named Darcy, the one who kidnapped Abby."

"You can't prove a thing. I want my lawyer. I'm entitled to a phone call," Sully said.

"I just caught you trying to put something in Leo's I.V. and I have a witness who can verify about Darcy. You are done and this is over," Jason said with hate in his eyes.

Sully just looked at him and said in a whisper so that only Jason could hear, "I might be done, but this ain't over."

Jason froze.

After the sheriff had someone set Sully's nose, he took him down to the station for interrogation. He set Sully in a room with nothing but a chair and a table with a phone on it. "Make your phone call. Keep it short," Sheriff Cooper said.

After Cooper left the room, Sully started dialing, "Carl, I need your help."

"Did you finish the job?" Carl asked.

"Before you go any further, I've been arrested and I'm sitting in an interrogation room."

"What the fuck are you calling me for?" Carl said, obviously pissed.

"I need an attorney. Isn't that what you do?" Sully asked.

"I can't be a part of this. I'll send you someone. Don't say a word until I have someone there with you. Keep your mouth shut!" Carl shouted.

"I ain't stupid!" Sully shouted back.

"Obviously you are. You got caught didn't you?" With that, Carl slammed the phone to disconnect.

Carl picked up his desk phone, "I need to speak to Mr. Ianareno."

"Who should I say is calling," a man said with a chuckle.

"Quit fucking around and put him on the phone!" Carl said.

"Calm down Carl, I'll get him."

"Yeah Carl, what do you need?" Mr. Mike Ianareno said calmly.

"Mike, who the hell did you send me? The fucker got caught and is now at a local police station," Carl said through gritted teeth.

"Take it easy!"

"Take it easy? That asshole called me from an interrogation room, asking for legal counsel," Carl replied.

"Sully is not stupid. He knows to keep his mouth shut. I've had him for over two years. I'll look into it and get back to you. Just sit tight," Mike said, and then hung up.

Jason went back to talk to the doctor about Leo.

"Doc, is Leo going to be alright?"

"Yes, he didn't even wake up which surprised me considering all the noise that was made. He is awake now, though. I had to wake him to check him over."

"When can I take him and Abby home?" Jason asked.

"I'd like to keep them over night. If they do well, you can take them both home tomorrow."

"By the way, Doc, did you find out what was in that needle that guy was trying to give Leo?"

"Yeah. Ricin, it's very toxic to humans. There was enough in there to kill him and then some. Had he succeeded, it would have been difficult to figure out. Thank God you caught him when you did."

"Thanks Doc," Jason replied, and then reached for his cell phone.

"Hey Coop, any chance you can send a couple guys

to guard Leo and Abby's room for the night? At least Leo's should be guarded. I'll be spending the night in Abby's room. Doc said that if all goes well, I can take them home tomorrow."

"No problem," Coop said, "I'll send someone there now."

"What's going on with the asshole?"

"Right now he is trying to lawyer up. It seems he's having a little trouble though. The guy he called brushed him off. Does the name Carl ring a bell?" Coop asked.

"Son of a bitch! Yeah. That's the guy I told you about that is in charge of Abby's inheritance," Jason said.

"I thought it sounded familiar. I'm glad that room isn't sound proof. Don't worry about this end. You take care of your family. If anything develops, I'll call you."

Jason headed back to Abby's room. He needed to be near her. He needed to know that she was safe and damn, he just needed to be with her to touch her, make contact to know that she was real and there. He opened her door and saw her sitting up looking at him with her big green eyes.

He went right over to her and grabbed her hand. He leaned over the bed to give her a kiss.

"Hey sweetheart, why are you sitting up?" he asked.

"I heard a loud noise and I heard you yelling and, and you weren't here…." She was visibly upset.

"It's all okay," he said as he gathered her in his arms. He climbed into the bed with her so he could hold her close and sooth her.

"Is Leo okay?" she asked, while placing her head on his chest.

"Yeah baby. He's okay. If you two are good through the night, I get to take you both home in the morning," Jason said, while rubbing her back. It felt so good to have her close; he never wanted to let her go.

"What was the loud bang, and why were you yelling?"

"Sully tried to poison Leo in his sleep, and I caught him?"

She leaned up and gasped, "How? Where did he

come from? How did he find us?" She was getting all worked up again.

"Shhh. It's going to be okay, baby. Sheriff Cooper has him down at the station. He won't be bothering anybody ever again. Leo is fine, the doctor checked him. He is sleeping. Something you should be doing if you want to go home tomorrow," Jason said softly while kissing her forehead, "We will have plenty of time to go over everything tomorrow when we get home."

"Are you going to stay with me?"

"Let anybody try to get me away from you," Jason said smiling down at her, "Shut your eyes baby, I'm not going anywhere."

Julia, Carl's wife, was walking down the hallway of their house when she heard her husband yelling into the phone and throwing things. She opened the door to his den and walked in.

"Are you going to talk to me and tell me what is going on? Hasn't the doctor warned you about your blood pressure? Do you want a heart attack?" Julia said as she stood there with her arms crossed over her chest.

"I should have taken care of the twins years ago when I had the chance," Carl said while punching the wall.

"Remember, if they didn't exist, there would have been no reason to have you as Abby's guardian," she said.

"Yeah, but I could have eliminated Leo in the beginning when I had him kidnapped from the hospital. Instead I hired some asshole heroin addict, and he botched the whole job up," Carl said with gritted teeth.

"Carl, you have to settle down. I know you don't like to worry me, but things have definitely gotten out of hand. I know more than you think I do. These walls are pretty thin, and I worry about you," Julia said softly, while massaging his shoulders, "We are a team, remember? Without you, I'd be lost. So let's just calm down and sort this out."

Julia and Carl talked for hours. She helped him find a

lawyer who could be trusted to keep his mouth shut, if the money was good enough. Carl called him and filled him in with as much as he needed to know in order to get paid, and get the job done.

Julia had known Abby's parents as well. In fact the four of them used to hang out together while going through college. Julia knew that Carl had held some animosity towards the Rinehearts, even back then. They had no idea that he felt that way, but she knew. She saw how Carl had to struggle to keep up, where as it seemed to come naturally to Abby's dad.

After Julia and Carl got married, she did her best to make him happy in spite of his jealousy. She made sure to keep their socializing to a minimum. She really loved Carl, and it hurt her to see him so twisted up inside.

After the car accident that killed Abby's parents, she was afraid that Carl would do something to harm Abby. She reminded him that he wouldn't get anything anyhow until the date of her 25th birthday, so just let her grow, and as she grew so would the interest in her inheritance grow. He agreed. When Abby turned 21, he started planning a way to remove her from getting in the way of the money. Julia knew that it was only a matter of time before he would do something permanent.

She convinced him to just let things lay low for a while, until this Sully mess was cleaned up. The money wasn't going anywhere for at least a year. He would concentrate on keeping his distance from Sully, so a connection could not be made between them.

Chapter 17

Light shined brightly into Abby's hospital room. Jason was still holding her against him. He looked down at her sleeping and said, "Wake up sleepy head. Don't you want to go home?"

She slowly opened her eyes, looked up at him and smiled.

"The doctor will be coming in soon to release you. I just saw him making his rounds," Jason told her.

Just then the doctor came in and did a double take when he saw Jason lying in bed with her.

"I think that is against hospital policy. I guess I better release you before you get into trouble," the doctor said with a smile.

"How's Leo?" Abby asked.

"I knew you would ask. I just came from him. He is itching to get out of here. So, if I can borrow your boyfriend for a few minutes, he can sign you two out of here. I need to go over some instructions with him about the both of you."

"I'll be right back, baby. Why don't you let the nurse start getting you ready to leave," he said, giving a quick peck on the cheek.

After going through all the necessary paperwork and getting Leo to reluctantly agree to be taken out in a wheelchair, Jason went to get his truck to take his family home. It felt so good to leave the hospital that the three of them couldn't wipe the smiles off their faces.

As soon as they were situated in the house, Jason had to remind them both, on several occasions, to take it easy. There would be plenty of time to take care of business. They were both eager to put Carl Pearlman into jail. So was Jason, but he wanted them healthy first.

They spent the next couple of days taking it easy and hanging around the house. Jason kept in contact with Dave and conducted his business from his home office. Things were running on schedule at the construction site, as he knew it would. His dad helped out on that end, and was kind of glad to do it. Jason knew his dad would get antsy just hanging around the house all the time. In fact, he was going to suggest that his dad come back part time to help out. He'd talk to him about it at the family Sunday dinner. Speaking of which, he just realized that he forgot to let his folks know that they were all back home. He better give mom a call.

"Hey mom! We are all back home," Jason said to his mother.

"Hi sweetheart! Glad to hear it. When did you get home?" she asked, "and how are they doing?"

"Just a couple days ago. Sorry I didn't call right away. I wanted to get everyone settled before making any phone calls," Jason replied, "They are both doing great. In fact it is hard to keep them from overdoing it."

"Think you all can make it to Sunday dinner?" she asked.

"That's the other reason I called. They are both eager to get out, so if you have enough for us all, we'll be there."

"When have we ever not had enough? I can't wait to see the three of you," his mom said.

"Want me to bring anything?"

"Just yourselves. I'll see you Sunday, son," she replied then hung up.

Since the day they all came home from the hospital, Abby insisted on staying in Jason's bedroom. She didn't want to be alone and she missed him terribly. For three nights, Jason, who normally slept naked, wore his sweatpants to bed. He knew he wouldn't be able to take it, let alone sleep, with skin to skin contact. It was hard enough just having her so close and smelling her scent; skin to skin was beyond his ability to control himself.

By the fourth night, Abby couldn't take it anymore. She reached down under the sheets, and started to rub his bare chest. Slowly she lowered her hand to go beneath his sweats, and grabbed his cock and squeezed. He was already hard to begin with.

"Abby, sweetheart, are you sure you're ready for this?" Jason asked. His heart was already beating rapidly.

"I've been ready. I'm not the one who took a bullet. All I did was give blood. I'm beginning to think that you're not attracted to me anymore," she said, while looking up at him with pouting lips.

"You know better than that," he answered. He rolled onto his side and pulled the sheet down. He then reached up under her pajamas and slowly ran his hand up her stomach, giving her one breast a gentle squeeze. He took his thumb and forefinger and gave the nipple a pinch and rolled it while watching her breath hitch.

She unbuttoned her top and pulled it off, throwing it on the floor.

"Someone a little anxious?" he said with a broad grin.

"Yeah. I need to feel you in me. I've missed you so much," she said, while placing her hand on his face and kissing him like she was starved.

He kissed her lips, then pressed her back onto the bed while kissing her neck. He gave her ear lobe a nip and lick. She turned her head to give him better access. His hands couldn't stop roaming over her body. He massaged one breast,

"Your breasts are perfect. They fill my hands just right and I love the way your nipples stand up when I lick them."

"I love the way your dick grows when I squeeze it," she said with a grin.

"At this point, you better stop squeezing or I'll be done before I get to enjoy your whole body," he said and removed her hand from his cock.

She gave him pouting lips, and he gave her a little chuckle then proceeded to lick and nip at one of her nipples. She groaned and ran her hand through his hair.

After the one nipple was thoroughly licked, he gently blew on it and it perked right up. Satisfied with a job well done, he proceeded to nip and lick the other nipple. She was starting to increase her breathing as every nip sent electric shocks straight to her clit.

He slid down the bed and pulled her PJ bottoms down. He just sniffed her pussy, looked up at her and smiled, "Your scent makes my dick grow also." Spreading her thighs farther apart with his shoulders he said, "Lay back and relax baby. Let me enjoy your sweet cream. We have all night."

With his thumbs he separated her folds. With his tongue, starting at the bottom of her pussy, he made a wide sweep up to her clit. She arched her back and gave a long groan. She ran her hands through his hair, and shoved his head against her mound. He smiled knowing that she was indeed enjoying this as much as he was. He took the tip of his tongue and flicked it over her nub; it made her shiver. Then he took her clit into his mouth and sucked on it. While sucking it, his tongue was flicking in and out. The sensation was too much and she gave a scream and jerked her hips as her back arched up. The orgasm was so strong she forgot to breath. She started bucking like a wild animal.
Jason looked up at her flush face and said, "Breathe sweetheart."

While she was still throbbing from her climax, he climbed up her body and slid his cock in her pussy. She gasped and wrapped her legs around his hips, not wanting him to pull out. He put a hand on each side of her head, and gave her a kiss that was so full of love and possession it made her dizzy. She could taste herself on his mouth, and that only excited her more. He pulled his cock out until the head would rub against her clit. This time when she groaned, he did too. His thrust was slow, and so was his tongue in her mouth. She ran her hands down his back and gave his ass cheeks a squeeze, then a gentle scratch with her nails. He knew he couldn't hold out much longer, her pussy held his dick with a vise grip. He slowly thrust in and out, in and out, over and over.

"Baby, your pussy is so hot and tight, fuck! You feel so good. I hope you are close, because I can't hold out much longer," he said while trying to grasp air.

"Go faster, Jason. Harder. Fuck me harder," she screamed at him.

He pumped faster. He could feel both their hearts beating together. He rose up on his forearms and started to piston in and out of her so fast, all that could be heard was smacking of sweaty flesh, as his balls hit her ass cheeks.

"Come Abby! Aaah. Shit! Fuuuuck!" Jason was yelling in wild throws of passion.

His words were enough to send her over the edge, and she bucked up with each of his thrusts. She could feel his hot jets of semen shoot inside of her. They both froze with her hips off the bed as she grabbed his penis with her inner muscles and squeezed every last drop of cum out of him. Then they both collapsed onto the bed, and Jason could feel her pussy spasm from her orgasm.

Jason didn't want to move, but he was afraid of being too heavy on her so he rested on his forearms. Her face was beautifully flush. He smiled down at her and kissed the tip of her nose. Rolling off of her, he hated pulling out of her. She felt so good, but he needed to hold her close to him.

"Are you okay honey? Did I hurt you?" Jason asked. He was running his hand through her hair while holding her against his chest.

"I might be shorter than you, but I'm not a piece of china. I don't ever recall having such strong orgasms before. Masturbation can't do that!" she said, while placing her chin against his chest and smiling up at him.

"I have to agree with you there. We seem to fit together just right, but I think we should practice a few billion more times just to make sure. Now that I know you're not a piece of china, maybe we can explore a few more of my fantasies," he grinned down at her, then wriggled his eyebrows.

"I guess you better marry me soon and make an honest woman out of me. After a billion times I won't be good for anyone else but you!" she said, then gave a yawn.

"Looks like I wore you out baby. We need to get some sleep anyhow. There is a lot to talk about in the morning."

The next morning, Abby snuck out of bed and went to the kitchen. She wanted to surprise her brother and Jason by making breakfast. She couldn't cook very well, no one really showed her how, but she could make a mean bowl of cereal with a side of toast and jam. She made coffee and set the table, complete with napkins and juice. She was quite proud of herself. She heard rustling upstairs, then the footsteps of two large men coming down the steps.

She stood proudly next to the well-made table and said, "I made my two best men breakfast."

"Well, look at that Jason. Our girl was busy this morning," Leo said, as he winked at her.

"You made my favorite! Toast, jam and coffee. The coffee smells great. Thanks babe."

He went right to her and hugged and kissed her.

They all sat and enjoyed breakfast. Abby was all smiles. This was probably the most normal she had felt since before her parents died. It was good. It was something that she wanted to have all the time. They lingered for a second cup of coffee, when Jason's phone rang. It was his mom.

"Hi mom, we just finished breakfast. What can I do for you?"

Jason stood and headed to the living room. He wanted to give Leo and Abby some alone time.

Leo looked up at Abby and said, "What can you tell me about Pearlman and his wife? Maybe if we compare notes, we can find a way to put an end to this."

"After mom and dad's deaths, I was sent away to a private school. The only time I came back was for holidays, and they weren't too festive. Most holidays I spent with neighbors, as the Pearlmans went up to their ski lodge."

"Sounds lonely," Leo said, and took her hand.

"It was, but at least I had a roof over my head and food in my mouth. From what you told me, you were lucky to sometimes have that. I can't imagine what it was like for you."

"It made me strong," Leo said. "What about Carl's wife? What is she like?" he asked.

"Julia? She's okay. Not too motherly though. I felt like I was intruding on her life when I did have to stay at their house. She wasn't mean or anything. She just made it clear that she only tolerated me."

"Do you think she knows what her husband is really like?" Leo asked.

"I don't really know. It's possible, she isn't mindless."

Jason walked back into the kitchen, "Mom just wanted to alert me that dad invited my crew for dinner on Sunday. It seems that they are concerned about us and, also, they want to go over some business matters."

"Will you be all day at your mom's?" Abby asked.
"Probably, but then again, so will you and Leo. Mom's is expecting the both of you. You're family now, and this is what family does," Jason said with a smile.

Neither of the twins had really had that before. Abby did growing up, but that seemed like a lifetime ago. It warmed both their hearts that not only did they find each other, but they now belonged to a loving family.

They continued to talk about the Pearlmans, trying to figure out a way to get Abby's inheritance away from them. Jason was planning to talk to Sheriff Cooper on Monday to see if he got anything out of Sully. With the odds firmly against Sully, maybe he'd be willing to strike a deal and give up Pearlman. For now though, he just wanted the three of them to relax a bit over the weekend and catch their breath. A lot had happened over the past few weeks. It was time to slow things down a bit.

Chapter 18

As they turned into Jason's parents' driveway, Leo and Abby noticed that there were cars everywhere, even on the front lawn. There had to be at least fifty people there. Jason led them through the front door, straight through the house to the back patio. When he opened the sliding glass door, all that could be heard was, "Uncle Jason!" Two little munchkins came running over and hugged his legs. Jason reached down and picked up his niece and nephew, giving them a sloppy kiss on the cheek.

"Ehhh, Uncle Jason, big boys don't kiss!" his three-year-old nephew, Little Jacob, said, while wiping it off with the back of his hand.

"I like your kisses Uncle Jason," said his five-year-old niece, Alice Louise, and gave him a hug around the neck. Jason introduced them to Leo and Abby, after which they wiggled and squirmed for Jason to put them down, so they could run off.

Jason looked up and saw that everyone was looking at them, so he smiled and waved, "Hi everybody! This is Abby, my fiancée and her twin brother, Leo."

In unison everybody yelled, "Hi Abby and Leo!"

Then they started to filter over to the three of them to welcome Abby and Leo. The twins were a little overwhelmed by all the attention. Jason led them around to the back yard, and introduced them to everyone. There were people in the big cement pool; they just waved and kept swimming. There were people playing horseshoes inviting Leo to join in with the other men, and Jason joined in with them. Abby was snatched up by Debbie, Jason's sister, and Jason's mom. Jason kept looking over at Abby to make sure she was comfortable. She seemed to be having a good time. Jason wasn't surprised; he knew how his family was. They went out of their way to make people feel comfortable.

He also knew that his family was relieved to see him happy again. They were all worried about him for so long because of Michelle's sudden death. He had been shaky for quite a while and only wanted to work or be alone. It took the whole family to get him there every Sunday, even if all he ever did was sit quietly in front of the television and stare at it without really listening.

The family never gave up on him. Abby was the answer to their prayers. There was no doubt that they would except her and love her. Leo, being her twin, would be accepted and loved also. Jason looked around trying to spot Leo, as well. He walked over to Abby and asked, "Where is Leo?"

"I thought he was with you guys playing horseshoes," Abby answered.

"He probably went inside. I'll go look for him. Are you okay?" Jason asked.

"What are you worried about big brother? You afraid I'll fill her in on your bad boy days?" Debbie said with a grin.

"Who, my Jason was a bad boy? I can't believe it! Dish it out sister, I need to hear this!" Abby replied with a huge grin.

Jason rolled his eyes and said, "Don't believe everything she says."

With that, he gave her a sweet kiss and left her with Debbie. He headed back into the house. He went into the kitchen where he found Leo talking to his cousin, Renee.

Renee Emerson was a looker, a tall, thin brunette, with blue eyes and a heart of gold. She grew up with Jason and Debbie. She had it a little rough. Her husband of only a year, Greg, had died in Iraq while under contract with the government. He was due to come home shortly and they wanted to start having kids. A roadside bomb put an end to that.

Afterward, Renee kept herself busy with her animals. She worked at an animal shelter. The family tried to set her up with dates, but she just wasn't interested or ready.

"So, I see you met my cousin Renee," Jason said to Leo, while planting a kiss on Renee's cheek.

"She was filling me in on her work with animals. She invited me to stop by sometime and she would show me around," Leo said smiling.

"That's a pretty good idea Renee. We could stand to have some normalcy. Is it alright if Abby and I join Leo next week sometime or is this a private tour?" Jason said to Renee with a wiggle of his eyebrows.

"Don't start Jas! I'd love to have the three of you come by. I work daylight shift, so just stop by when you guys have time," she said.

"Well, since I can't start any trouble here, I'm going back outside to play horseshoes with dad. Catch you guys later," Jason said, and left them alone to talk.

When he turned back around before heading to the back yard, the two of them were laughing. It was so good to see the both of them having a good time. He hoped something would blossom between them.

While throwing horseshoes, his crew gathered around him. They talked about shop as they played. Things were running smoothly now that Darcy was out of the picture. Dave mentioned that they were going to do a more thorough background check with any new hires. They still could use a couple new guys, as orders where backing up. Jason suggested that Dave check with Leo. If he was interested, that would be fine by him.

By nightfall, everyone started to filter out. Leo and Renee were still hanging together, sitting on the grass under a tree, off by themselves. Abby was circled by the ladies of the family talking wedding stuff. Just then Jason spotted Coop coming around the house heading toward him. Abby and Leo headed over as well.

"What's up Coop?" Jason asked.

"I hate crashing the family get-together, but I need to talk to you, Abby, and Leo," Sheriff Cooper said, as Abby walked up behind him. Leo looked over from where he was talking to Renee.

"Let's go inside to dad's study. It will be more private," Jason said as he waved Leo over.

They all went inside the house to the study. Jason shut the

door and locked it so that they wouldn't be disturbed.

"Okay Coop, what's going on?" Jason said, as they each took a seat.

"This is going to be a little surprising; it was to me. Sully is an FBI informant," Coop said.

They all looked at him like he was nuts, with eyes wide and chins dropped.

"Get the fuck out," Leo remarked.

"My sentiments exactly," Jason said.

"How's that possible? He was hunting me down in the woods to kill me. He killed Darcy!" Abby said.

"First off Abby, if he would have found you, he wouldn't have killed you. He would have called for back up to come and get you. Leo, he just meant to graze you but you shifted into the bullet," Coop said. "As for Darcy, Sully's claiming self-defense. Me, I believe he just hated the murderous son-of-a-bitch after what he saw him do to you, Abby."

"How do you explain the ricin? I saw him. He was going to poison Leo," Jason said.

"He saw you heading to the room. That was staged. He had to get caught in order to not blow his cover. By the way Jason, he said that you pack quite a wallop. He never would have gave the poison to Leo, but he didn't know how else to make sure that Carl would know that he did indeed try to kill you two," Coop said.

"But why? Why is the FBI interested in us?" Abby asked.

"They're not; they are interested in Carl Pearlman. He seems to be connected to the Ianareno mob family, and that is what Sully was working on when Carl called Mr. Ianareno and asked for an assassin for hire. It was the break that they were waiting on," Coop answered.

"Where is Sully now?" Leo asked.

"He is still in lock up, but he is using this time to fill in his superiors. If the scum bag of a lawyer that Carl sent him can't find an angle to get him out, his cover will be done and he'll have to pull out. Meanwhile, you two will have to stay put with Jason. You both are still a target. Sully does believe that Carl will try to find someone else to finish the job. He did tell me that they do have eyes and ears on both Pearlman and Ianareno. This might be enough to make the connection and bring them both down. That's all I have for now, but nothing can leave this room. Any leaks could blow Sully's cover and put you all in danger."

"We all understand," Jason spoke for the three of them, "You will keep us in the loop?"

"When I know something, you'll know something," Coop said, then stood to leave.

"You are here already. I'm sure mom and dad will want you to stay and have a bite to eat. Dad is probably still horse shoeing it," Jason said.

"I'd like to, but I need to get back. That lawyer is still hanging around, and I need to see if he is up to something. Give your folks my regards," he said as he shook Jason and Leo's hand. He looked over at Abby and said, "You stay close to these two. No running off on your own."

"I have nowhere to go. Those two are my home now," Abby said.

The three of them went out back after Sheriff Cooper left. Leo zeroed in on Renee, and walked over her way. Jason grabbed Abby's hand and said, "You look tired babe. You want to leave soon?"

"Whenever you are ready to leave, so am I. I don't think we should leave right away or your parents will think it had something to do with the sheriff talking to us. I'll go hang out with the girls for about an hour," Abby said looking up at him, and giving him a smile.

"Maybe one more game of horseshoes with dad, then we can leave. Leo seems to be enjoying himself with Renee. Think something is developing there?" Jason asked.

"Maybe. I hope so. After the talks we have had, his life has been pretty lonely. He could use a woman's gentle touch. What's Renee like?"

"She's good people. I think they would be good for each other. Speaking of a woman's touch, I could use some of yours," Jason said with a grin and a wiggle of his eyebrows.

"Down tiger. You still have a game of horseshoes with your dad to get through. I'll go over and let Leo know our plans. Maybe he'll want to stay longer. Think Renee could ride him home?"

"If she can't, someone will. Don't worry about it, sweet pea. Go talk wedding stuff with mom and Debbie. I know they are enjoying the hell out of that."

He gave her butt a love tap and walked over to his dad.

Debbie was anxious to talk wedding. She had all kinds of ideas for Abby. Seeing her brother so happy and in love warmed her heart. Debbie took to Abby right away. They connected like they'd known each other for years.

"Abby, do you want a big wedding or just something simple," Debbie asked.

"I'm not much for big to-dos, In fact, this size group is quite overwhelming for me. I'd be happy with something just like this here in the backyard, if that's okay with you Mrs. Donahue?" Abby asked Jason's mom.

"Oh, sweetheart. Either call me mom or if you are not ready for that, call me Louise. Everyone calls me mom or gran. I'd be honored to help put something together with you here on our property," she said as she gave Abby a hug.

"Okay then," Debbie said, "we can start planning. Mom, how about you, me and Abby going to lunch next Wednesday? That will give me some time to jot down some ideas. What do you think Abby?"

"That's sounds great to me. I have one question though," Abby shyly put her head down.

"Ask away," Debbie said.

"I know you haven't known me very long, but I feel like I've known you for a long time. Would you be my maid of honor?"

Debbie smiled. With tears in her eyes she said, "I thought you would never ask! I was hoping. Yes, I'd love to."

Jason came walking over.

"What's all this hugging and crying going on over here?"

"I was just asked to be the maid of honor at your

wedding. Now I can keep an eye on you all through the ceremony. How about them apples, big brother?" Debbie said, smiling.

"You think you know all my tricks, but, sis, I still have a few up my sleeve. I sort of figured Abby would ask you. I can't think of anyone better," Jason gave his sister a peck on the cheek, "Are you ready to go Abby? It has been a long day. I'm sure you're pretty tired by now."

"We'll pick you up around ten on Wednesday, sweetheart," Louise said.

As they walked over to Leo, Jason asked, "What's on Wednesday?"

"Girl's lunch to make wedding plans," Abby said with a wide grin, "Want to come?"

"No thank you! I'll leave that to you girls. You just tell me where and when, and I'll be there with bells on my toes. And Abby, make it soon. I want you as my wife, yesterday. The sooner the better. In fact, if you want, we could fly to Vegas next weekend," he said, putting his arm around her shoulder bringing her in for a kiss.

"Your mom and sister would be sooo disappointed. They are really looking forward to this. I couldn't do that to them," she said.

"Hey Leo, we are heading out now. Are you coming or staying?" Jason asked.

Leo looked over at Renee.

"I could drop you off on my way home, if you'd like," Renee offered.

"Yes, I'd like," Leo said, all smiles, "You guys go on. I'll catch up with you later."

Chapter 19

On the way home, Jason mentioned that he would be driving her to Wednesday's lunch. He didn't want to say anything in front of his mom or sister. Until things were under control, and there were no more threats to her life, he would be driving her everywhere. Hopefully that wouldn't be too much longer.

Abby really didn't mind it, though. It was nice to have someone care so much about her. She hadn't had that since her parents died. Anyhow, she loved being with Jason and wanted to be with him as much as possible. It had dawned on her on the ride home that, since Leo hadn't come with them, they would have the whole house to themselves. She smiled. She turned her head to look at Jason as he was driving, he was smiling also.

"Are you thinking what I'm thinking?" Jason asked.

"What are you thinking?" she asked.

"That we will have the whole house to ourselves for a while," he said.

"Yep," was all she said.

She then took her hand and slowly ran it up his thigh. While looking for his reaction, she palmed his erection, "Feels like you have plans."

"Yep," he said, as he pulled into his driveway.

He no sooner parked than he jumped out of his truck, ran around to Abby's door, and lifted her out. He carried her while running for the front door. He wanted to kiss her then, but was afraid he'd trip on the porch steps. It seemed to take forever to get the front door open, but when he did he kicked it closed with his foot. While still holding her, he had her reset the alarm. They got as far as the stairs and he couldn't wait any longer, he devoured her mouth with his. She wrapped her arms around his neck. He placed her on the steps and started tearing her clothes off. She grabbed his shirt, ripped it open and buttons flew everywhere.

"Baby, all I could think about all day was being inside you. Do you know how hard it was to keep my dick from making a fool of me? I'm exhausted!" Jason said, as he grabbed one of her nipples with his mouth and sucked.

"My poor baby," Abby replied.

Abby nudged him so she could reach down and unbuckle his jeans. She then pushed both his jeans and underwear down to let his cock spring free. She grabbed his shaft and felt its' heavy, steel hardness. Jason hissed through clenched teeth. Looking between them she saw his cock's purplish head swell with her touch.

"That looks a little painful, my poor neglected baby," Abby cooed.

Jason pushed her hand away, and quickly gathered her up. Taking two steps at a time, he ran upstairs as his dick bobbed up and down. Abby wrapped her arms around his neck and was kissing his neck.

When he got to the bedroom, he plopped her down on the center of the bed and dove on top of her.

"I hope you are as ready as me because this is going to be fast and hard," Jason said through gritted teeth.
It was taking everything in him not to come all over her.

"Fuck me Jason! Hurry. Fuck me hard!" she said in between gasps of air.

She spread her legs with her knees up and spread her pussy lips for him. He didn't even have to position himself; his penis knew where home was. In one thrust he was in and filled her completely. He stayed that way for a minute, wanting to feel her warmth. Her pussy grabbed his penis repeatedly.

"Aaah baby, you are so tight. I can feel your pussy is swollen. Shit, fuck…it's grabbing me. I don't know if I can even move," Jason gasped.

Abby pulled her hips back and ground into him. His eyes rolled back. They both groaned.

"Jason! Faster! Please….faster, harder….I'm on the edge," Abby cried breathily.

Jason pulled back all the way until only the head of

his cock was in. Then he drove it home, and they both groaned again. He picked up his pace and thrust faster, pistoning in and out, with his balls smacking her ass cheeks. The sound of sweaty flesh smacking sweaty flesh echoed in the room.

Hearing Jason's groan was all she needed. She came with a loud yell, as her climax ripped through her body. Her hips bucked automatically in time with each of his thrusts. Her yell sent Jason off and he yelled, "aaaah fuck……Abby! I'm coming!"

He pumped into her one more time and held as he shot his load. She could feel his warm cum shooting all the way inside her. That made her come again and she bucked her hips and milked him dry.

They both laid still gasping for air as sweat made their bodies stick together. Jason leaned up on his forearms and looked down at her face. He kissed her nose and smiled.

"Will I ever be able to go slow with you?" he asked.

"I don't think either of us will on the first round," she answered up at him.

"Does that mean we can have a second round?" he asked, while wiggling his eyebrows.

"We can have as many rounds as we can handle, but can we have a quick shower first?"

"Good idea….for round two!"

Abby slapped his ass cheek. She wiggled her body for him to move. When he rolled on his side, she squirmed out of bed and made a bee line, as much as possible with legs of rubber, to the bathroom.

She turned around and smiled saying, "Round two, coming up!"

Jason jumped up and chased her to the bathroom. By the time they finished making love again in the shower, and then actually taking a shower, Abby felt like a pile of Jell-O. Jason dried her off, and carried her to bed. She loved how his muscles flexed when he held her. There wasn't an ounce of fat on him. Her favorite thing to do was to look at and touch his body. She could tell that his muscular physique came from all the hard work he did, and not from spending hours at a gym. Just the way she liked it. She laid her head on his chest, he covered them both, then just wrapped his arms around her. A few minutes later, she was out like a light.

Jason just held her, listening to her gentle breaths. He couldn't believe how lucky he was to have her. He loved her so much, it made his heart hurt.

As he stared out his bedroom window into the night, he wondered how he was supposed to keep her safe with a mad man hiring hit men to kill her and her twin brother. He was at a loss. He was hoping that Sully could produce enough proof to put Pearlman in jail, but would he? The FBI didn't want just Pearlman, they wanted the Ianareno family, as well. Would Sully's information be enough? That's what he was hoping. Looking down at his sleeping Abby, he smiled again and closed his eyes to try to sleep.

Morning came too soon. Jason hardly slept. Abby stretched like a content cat beside him, then rolled onto her side.

Looking up at him she said, "Mornin' handsome. Want me to make my famous cinnamon toast?"

"That sounds great. Afterwards, how about we head over to my office and check on things. Would you like to start on my books?" he asked, and started to get up.

"I guess I better before you fire me," she said.

"Sweetheart, I could never fire you. Now what kind of future husband would I be if I did that?" giving her a peck on the cheek.

Heading down toward the kitchen, they both noticed that Leo hadn't come home all night.

"I guess Leo and Renee hit it off," Abby said.

"I think they would be good for one another. You'll like Renee. She is a real sweetheart. I'll give her a call later this afternoon, after we leave the office."

As Jason brewed coffee, Abby made them toast. They no sooner sat down when they heard the front door open.

"I smell coffee!" Leo yelled from the doorway.

"Well, look what the cat dragged in," Jason said.

Leo headed straight for the coffee; "So, what's on the agenda for today?" Leo asked, completely ignoring Jason's comment.

"How's Renee?" Abby asked, winking at Leo and smiling.

"Okay guys. Knock it off. Wipe those grins off your faces. Renee is fine. All we did is talk all night," Leo said.

"It don't matter to me what you two do, just don't hurt her. She's had enough heartache. She's good people, Leo. I can see the two of you hitting it off," Jason said.

"You don't have to tell me. She already has me wrapped around her baby finger. Just don't tell her that. We are getting together again this evening. Hey, where are you guys heading," Leo asked.

"Down to my office. Why?"

"Mind if I come? Dave offered me a job, and if it is alright with you, I'd like to take him up on it," Leo replied.

Jason smiled, "I'm the one who suggested it. You'll like my crew, and you'll fit in just fine."

With that, they all headed out.

Chapter 20

Carl's phone rang. "Hello," he said.

"Carl, its Mike. Listen up. I just heard from Sully, and he is heading back. Until the situation cools down, your request has to wait," Mike replied.

"I already paid you. I need these hits done!" Carl yelled in the phone.

"You have about a year to take care of it. It is bringing too much heat down on the family business. In fact, I think we should cut ties for just a bit," Mike said.

"How can you do that? I take care of the ledgers," Carl answered.

"Watch your mouth. Your lines could be tapped. Just hold on to things for now. I'll call you when I think it is safe," Mike replied, then hung up.

"Son of a bitch!" Carl yelled, and threw his phone.

Julia entered the den, "What's going on?"

"Mike is cutting me out for a while, until things cool down. I know he has a shipment of drugs coming next week. I put it in the ledgers. How can I keep accurate records being out of the loop? Now he wants me to wait to complete my business with the twins, as well."

"You do have some time for that. Abby's 25th birthday is almost a year away. What's the hurry?" Julia asked.

"I didn't want it to happen close to that time, so as to not bring suspicion. I have no choice now," Carl remarked while hitting his desk.

"Calm yourself down. It will work out. Mike didn't say he wouldn't take care of the hits on the twins, did he? He just wants to play it safe," she said.

"Did you get that?" asked FBI agent Thomas listening to the bug that Sully planted in Carl's office.

"Yeah. What a scumbag. I better report this in. I just wish he would have given more information on the drug shipment," agent Reilly replied.

They were both in a van about a half a block away. The van had bogus markings advertising a key making shop. They had been parking in various locations near Carl's house since Sully planted the bug.

Chapter 21

The crew was still sitting around the small break room. Dave was passing out assignments. The guys looked up when the three of them entered.

"Hey, the boss decided to grace us with his company," one of them said, and they all snickered.

Jason just smiled and said, "I missed you guys too. Fill me in on the sites, Dave. Oh, by the way, meet your new crew member, Leo. And guys, don't be too hard on him, he's my future brother-in-law."

The guys each gave Leo a nod and a pat on the back, welcoming him to the group. Dave assigned Leo to go with one of the more experienced men to learn the ropes. As the crew headed out, Dave stayed behind to catch Jason up to date, and to tell him that he found a Manila envelope in the mailbox marked with his name. He had placed it on Jason's desk. After that, he left also.

Jason showed Abby where she would be working. His office building was just one floor but had plenty of space with a break room, small kitchen, two restrooms, a small reception area that consisted of a desk, old leather couch, and a few stuffed chairs. The whole front of the building was glass, including the glass and metal door that read: "Donahue Construction". The floors were light tan tile, and the walls were medium brown wood panel. The hallway off to the side of the reception area led back to the other rooms. Jason's office was at the end of the hall. It was the largest room, with plenty of seating. There were two large leather couches with matching stuffed chairs, and two large conference tables. His desk was just as grand, being a dark mahogany wood. There was a door off to the side that led into his bookroom. That was where Abby would work. She had her own desk, chair, phone and bathroom. The desk was average size. It was heaped with books and scattered papers. Although her room was small, it was airy. It had two large picture windows to allow light in.

"Where do I start?" Abby said more to herself than Jason.

"I know it's a mess. See how much I need you?" he said with a smile.

"I'm going to have to organize everything first before I can even start on the books," Abby said.

"However you want to do it is fine with me. I'm thrilled that you will even try to tackle this mess. If you need anything, just yell. I'll do my best not to bother you," Jason said, watching her disappear behind a stack of papers.

He walked back to his desk chair and noticed the envelope that Dave had mentioned. He picked it up and saw it had no return address. It was firmly sealed shut. He opened the envelope with a knife and pulled out a typed letter that said:

"You can't protect her all the time, and you certainly cannot protect them both. It doesn't concern you. Stay out of it, or you will be added to the list."

Jason called Dave, "Dave, where's Leo?"

"He's with Rick. Why?"

"That envelope you put on my desk? It was a warning and a threat to Abby and Leo's life. Abby is with me. I haven't told her yet. Fill Leo in, and make sure he is never left alone. I'm going to give Coop a call. Let me know if anything is off. Tell Leo that I want him back here pronto, and don't let him come here alone. Got it?" Jason said.

"I'll bring him personally. See you in a few."

Jason stood up to look in on Abby. She was engrossed in her work. He walked in quietly, went to her windows, and shut the blinds. Because they were at street level, it would be easy for someone to see her and try to take a shot.

"Hey! I need that light! What's the big idea?" she asked with her fists on her waist.

"Sorry honey, you're a sitting duck with these

windows. I'll get the guys to put in more fluorescent lighting for you. Meanwhile, I have some desk lamps in storage. I'll go get them," he said, and headed to the storage room two doors down the hall.

Abby followed behind him, "What has you so edgy?"

"Just being cautious."

"The look on your face says otherwise. C'mon Jason, what's going on?"

She stopped him and placed her hands on his forearms while staring into his eyes.

"That envelope that Dave told me about? It contained a threat. Don't worry, I already called Dave and he is bringing Leo here. I'm going to call Coop now," he said.

He hated to even tell her. He so much didn't want to worry her, but at the same time, if he was going to keep her safe, she had to know what was going on. After setting her up with lights, he gave Coop a call and filled him in on the note.

"I already know about it. I was heading over to talk to the three of you. You at the office?" Coop asked.

"What do you mean you knew about it? I just got it this morning."

"I'll explain when I get there," Coop said, and hung up.

Abby kept working. It helped to keep her calm. When Leo walked into his office, Jason filled Leo in on the note. Sheriff Cooper wanted to talk to all three of them. Leo took a seat on one of the couches, and started to read a magazine. Jason paced the floor, and kept looking in on Abby. Half the time he couldn't see her behind the stacks of files and papers, but he heard her shuffling around. Twenty minutes later, Coop came walking in.

"Abby, sweetheart, would you please put on a pot of coffee? I have a feeling we are going to need it," Jason said.

"Sure. Don't start without me," she said, and headed for the break room.

"Let me see the letter, Jason." As he was examining it, Abby came back in.

"Coffee will be ready in about ten minutes. Did I miss anything?"

"No. We are just getting started," Jason answered.

They all gathered around one of the conference tables. Leo was quiet but calm. Abby couldn't sit still. Jason couldn't even stay seated.

"What's going on Coop? How did you know about this letter? What happened with Sully?" Jason was firing questions left and right.

"Calm down; one thing at a time. Sully dropped the envelope off," Coop said.

"What the hell?" Jason said. Leo stared at Coop with a confused look, as did Abby.

"He had to keep his cover. After that low life lawyer that Pearlman sent got him off on a technicality, he had to make a call in to Mike Ianareno to let him know that he got away with it, and was heading back. Ianareno dictated that letter and told him to deliver it before he left town."

"I'm curious. Humor me here. What was the technicality?" Leo asked.

"He was hunting deer when he accidentally dropped his rifle and it went off," Coop said with a wince.

"Twice? What, he dropped his rifle two times? One bullet went above Abby's head and one went in my shoulder. What the fuck!" Leo said, still sitting.

"This was what Sully's government boss told him to say to the lawyer in order for the lawyer to have something to fall back on," Coop said.

"Doesn't Sully have enough on these guys to put them away?" Abby asked.

"Good question," Jason agreed.

"This is probably enough to get Pearlman, but he isn't the big fish they are really after. They have been suspecting this mob family of drug trafficking. There is rumor of another delivery coming up in the near future. That is why Sully had to go back under. They have Pearlman's house bugged, thanks to Sully, and that has been very helpful. They are very close to shutting them all down, but it may take a few more weeks," the sheriff said.

"A few more weeks? What about Abby and Leo's safety?" Jason asked.

"The agency is aware of your predicament. Jason, they asked me if you could hide them somewhere until this is broken wide open. I was thinking. What if the three of you went to your dad's fishing lodge in the mountains?" Coop asked.

"Not a bad idea," Jason said.

"I'm sure your dad and Dave can take care of the business for a while. I'll give you a secure cell phone, and take only it. All others might be traced. You might want to take your hunting gear also, for protection, just in case. Also, you can't tell anyone where you are going," Coop said.

"Jason, I don't want to leave Renee. This is the first time I have ever considered having a relationship with a woman. If I go, I want to take her also," Leo said.

"If she wants to go, that's fine with me, but we leave tonight," Jason said.

Coop looked at all three of them and said, "One more thing. There are going to be two agents following you, agents Reiley and Thomas. They will follow from a distance to make sure you are not being followed. I just wanted you aware of that. Jason call me and let me know that you made it okay. I'll let your dad know that I sent you out of town for safety reasons."

Abby just listened quietly. As long as Jason was with her, she didn't care where they went.

Jason's dad, Jacob, had a remote fishing lodge in the Brushy Mountains in North Carolina. The area is a "spur" of the Blue Ridge Mountains. The lodge was in Pores Knob in Wilkes County, which is the highest point of the mountains and was very secluded. Jacob also had a fishing boat on the nearby Catawba River. He used to take Jason fishing several times a year until Jason enlisted. Jason knew the area like the back of his hand.

Chapter 22

That evening, the four of them headed out. It would take several hours to get there. Jason couldn't see anyone following them, but he knew the agents were out there somewhere.

By the time they hit the mountains, it was very dark. There were several dirt roads, and unless a person knew where they were going, they'd be lost in minutes, especially in the dark. There were many forks in the road. Jason had no problem knowing which way to go. It was quiet in the truck just about the whole way until he pulled up to the lodge. It was quite impressive. It was made of logs and stone with a huge glass bay window in the front.

Leo whistled, "Holy shit! This place is huge and in the middle of nowhere!"

Jason smiled, "Wait until you see the inside."

They all jumped out, grabbing gear, and followed Jason to the front door. Walking into the foyer, they were greeted by a huge stuffed black bear that looked like he could eat someone. The ladies jumped and gasped.

"That's dad's security bear. He had it stuffed in attack mode in case someone tried to break in at night. Don't worry, he doesn't bite," Jason smiled. Abby hit his arm.

The foyer led to a large living room with a stone fireplace. The mantle to the fire place had family pictures on it. Many were pictures of Jason and his family throughout the years. Abby could pick him out in every one. Two stuffed dark brown leather couches lined either side of the room. Two matching stuffed leather recliners faced the fireplace with end tables on both sides. Matching coffee tables sat in front of each couch. The living room was enormous, but still had a very warm quality to it. It looked comfortable.

"Come on, I'll give you the grand tour," Jason said, as he led them to the kitchen area.

His dad kept the place stocked, just in case he needed a break and wanted to fish. The kitchen was equipped with all the modern appliances. The refrigerator was a wide, side by side two door. A couple of whole deer could fit in it! The cabinets were all dark wood grain, and the counters were marble. The table was wood also and could seat eight people, easily. There was a small pantry off to the side that held a washer and dryer that made doing laundry very convenient.

Beside the kitchen was a dining room that looked like it wasn't used very much. The dining room table could seat eight people comfortably. The other side of the dining room led into a small den. The floor plan went in a complete circle that led back to the living room.

At the end of the foyer, steps led up to a huge loft. Behind the loft were three bedrooms, each had their own bathroom. The loft had a large hot tub right in the center, so that when someone was in it, they could see outside through the bay windows of the living room. The place was peaceful and inviting to say the least.

"I wouldn't mind living here, Jason. This place is beautiful," Abby said.

"Thanks, Jas, for letting me tag along. I haven't had a vacation in years. Get a load of this hot tub!" Renee said.

"Let's get settled in, first. Then we can meet up in the kitchen and discuss plans," Jason said, heading to the master bedroom with Abby.

Renee looked at Leo and smiled, then nodded for him to follow her to one of the other bedrooms. He didn't have to be asked twice.

After unpacking, they all went into the kitchen.

"First things first. No one is to go anywhere outside alone. Girls, I'd prefer if you got me or Leo to escort you outside," Jason remarked, "We have to stay sharp while we are here, and Leo and I both have weapons. We will use them if necessary. Any objections?"

"No," all three said in unison.

"Now, if you are all up for it, I can fill the hot tub, and we can all soak while we discuss tomorrow. I have a few ideas and want to make sure you guys are up for it. What do you say?" Jason asked.

"I think that is a splendid idea. Naked or clothed," Leo asked while facing Renee.

"I'm not ready to see you naked, brother," Abby said, "I vote clothes. We all brought our swim gear anyhow."

Jason and Leo just chuckled. They didn't have a problem with the naked thing. Leo figured that he would be busy with Renee, and probably wouldn't even pay attention to his sister, but they all agreed to meet at the hot tub in swim suits.

Jason started the hot tub while the others went to change. While he was tending to that, the cell phone that Coop gave him rang.

"Jason here," Jason said.

"I thought I asked you to call me as soon as you got there?" Coop asked.

"I was going to as soon as I got the hot tub filled. All is okay for now. Any news at your end?" Jason asked.

"Sully told his superiors that something is on the horizon. They are close, Jason. You just keep everyone safe for now. I let your dad in with minimum info. Your mom and sister were getting worried because Abby didn't make their lunch date. Your dad will let them know that you all had to leave in a hurry for safety reasons," Coop said.

"I hope they will settle for that now. My sister can be pretty nosey when it concerns family. I'm planning on taking us all on the boat tomorrow to the supply store. I'll keep the cell with me. Call if anything develops," Jason said.

"Will do, son. You stay safe. I'll call tomorrow evening just to touch base," Coop said, then hung up.

The four of them slipped into the tub. Leo was the first to ask, "Was that Coop?"

"Yeah. He was just checking on us. No news as of yet," he said to Leo.

He smiled when all he heard was moans of pleasure coming from the girls. He made sure that the water was toasty.

"Ahhh, this is great!" Renee said. "My bones needed this."

"I second that ahhh!" replied Abby with a huge grin. She then asked, "What are we going to do tomorrow?"

"Well," Jason started, "I was thinking we could head down to the dock to my dad's fishing boat, and I'll take you all down the river to a little town on the opposite bank. We can get any supplies we need, and you girls can look around. There is a great bar and grill there where we can grab some lunch. How does that sound?" Jason said.

"You'd make a great cruise director," Leo said with a grin.

"Smart shit!" Jason answered, then gave Leo a shove.

"Oooh! Shopping! What do you say Abby?" Renee asked.

"I'm happy with anything. This alone has been more than I could ever expect or hope for," she said, and meant every word.

Everyone went quiet.

"Babe, I know you are scared and worried. Leo and I will do our best to keep you safe. You are my life now, and I'll give my all to keep you happy," Jason said, and kissed her.

"He is right, sis. It won't always be like this. Hopefully Sully will have enough to put that bastard Carl away for life. I know how you feel. I'm sick of running and looking over my shoulder, too," Leo said. "Jason, I like that boat idea, but any reason why we can't sleep in a bit first?"

"Sure, we can sleep in. How about we gather in the kitchen say eleven o'clock?" Jason asked.

They all agreed. They spent another couple hours in the tub then headed to their bedrooms. All four agreed that it had been a long day, and they were all exhausted. The next day would be busy, but it would be a fun busy.

Once Renee and Leo shut their bedroom door, Renee headed to the bathroom. Leo stripped then plopped himself on the bed face down. Renee came into the bedroom wearing a black see-through nightie. She quietly tipped toed over to the bed and gave Leo a slapped on the ass.

"That's a good way to get your own ass spanked," Leo said, then looked up and saw Renee, "God woman, you look beautiful. Come here and let me hold you."

With the black nightie and her long dark hair, her skin looked soft and white. Her eyes sparkled an aqua blue color. Just looking at her gave Leo an enormous erection. Renee stared at it and licked her lips.

"Ahhh baby, don't look at it that way. I want to have some control here. It has definitely been a while since I've done this," Leo said, as Renee slowly climbed into bed.

"Me too," Renee said. As soon as she rested in Leo's arms, she looked up and said, "Are you packing protection?"

"Jason handed me a handful. Said he doesn't need them with Abby. I told him I didn't want to hear it, then took them off his hands," Leo said with a big grin.

"Jas, you got to love him," Renee said, then reached down between them and grabbed his cock. "You're so big and hard. I want to taste you."

"You are killing me here, babe," Leo said, then gave her access to him.

Renee looked up at him while she slowly licked her way down his chest. She bit each of his nipples, and he shivered. Smiling, she lowered herself between his legs, then got up on her knees and lowered her head down to his inner thigh. She licked him then licked his balls. Running her tongue up his steel hard shaft, she popped the head into her mouth. She looked up at Leo and saw him looking down at her with gritted teeth, hissing breath, trying to keep control. She smiled knowing she was exciting him. Sucking in with her mouth, she slowly sucked down his shaft taking him to the back of her throat and swallowed.

"Aaahhh, Fuck...Renee! Your mouth is so hot and wet. It's been too long, babe. I'll come and I don't want to yet. I want our first time to be with me in you," Leo said, then he reached down, pulled her up and climbed on top of her. "As beautiful as your nightie is on you, it has to go," he said, and then pulled it off of her.

Thank God she wasn't wearing the thong that went with it. He could barely put on a condom without ejaculating. He spread her pussy lips and felt. She was soaked, ready for him. He spread her and eased his penis in slowly; he didn't want to hurt her. It took all his willpower not to just ram her to the hilt. One inch at a time he entered her. He looked up at her to see her eyes glazed over, so he kissed her and they both groaned into each other's mouth as he fully seated inside her. They both went still, acclimating to each other. Renee raised her legs and rubbed her heals over his ass. "Leo, you make me feel so full. I need you to move ...oooh, please, aahhh...you feel hard and good. Fuck me Leo, fuck me hard!" she said into his ear, then bit down on his shoulder while running her finger up his back.

Leo pulled out with just the head of his penis left inside and moved quick, short thrusts until she pushed on his ass for more. He rose up then drove in, all the way. His jaw hurt from gritting his teeth in order not to come. Again he pulled out. They were both gasping for air and sweat covered the both of them.

"More Leo. Fuck me! Faster.....I'm so close....aaaahhh," Renee cried.

Leo couldn't hold on anymore. He rose up and started to piston in and out of her, over and over. Their bodies made a sucking sound as they met. Flesh smacking flesh. The sound alone sent them both over the top.

"Aaaah....fuck... me! Babe....your pussy is clenching me. Come for me, come now!" Leo said as he reared up. He felt her climax just as he shot into the condom. He wished the damn thing wasn't there. He wanted to shoot into her, filling her with his cum. Renee shivered as her climax made her pussy swell and throb. She couldn't get enough air as she gasped. Their heartbeats thumped rapidly together. Leo realized that he was crushing her, so he rolled onto his side and gathered her in his arms.

"You okay," he asked in between breaths.

"I needed that," she said with a grin, "I hope I wasn't too loud."

"You were great! Your screams were so sexy, if they heard you, you probably got them both off," Leo said while kissing her forehead.

"By the way," Renee said, "maybe I want a spanking."

"Why you kinky little minx. I'll remember that for next

time," Leo said.

They laid there quietly, just holding each other, catching their breath. Leo couldn't even remember the last time he had a woman in his arms. It felt so good. Renee felt so right. Things needed to calm down if he wanted to start a life with her, and he knew that. Whatever it took, he was going to see that he and his sister could have a happy and normal life. Renee was his. She might not know it yet, but he did.

It didn't take long for the both of them to fall asleep in each other's arms.

Chapter 23

"Carl, this is me. The new shipment of goods is coming in next Thursday, around eight at night. I need you to be ready with the ledgers," Mike said.

"I thought you were cutting me out," Carl answered.

"Well I'm cutting you back in, smart ass! Anyhow, the twins are out of the picture for now," Mike said.

"What do you mean by that?" Carl asked

"Just what I said. They are gone. Can't be found anywhere. That Donahue guy left and took them somewhere. None of my guys can find a trace on them. Maybe now things will cool down, and we can get back to business. If you want your cut, do your job," Mike said, and hung up.

"Shit! Now what am I going to do?" Carl said to himself.

He figured that if Mike's men couldn't find the twins, nobody could. How could he get rid of them if he couldn't even find them? He knew he still had time, but the sooner the better. He wanted to be done with all of this, then he could take his wife and move out of the country, be done with everybody, especially the Ianareno family. For the time being, he knew he better tend to the ledgers if he wanted the money it would bring. Then he had an idea.

He called Mike back. "Mike, how about sending a guy to the Donahue Construction. Have the guy sign on for work, then he can snoop around and see if he can find out anything," Carl said.

"You're a pain in my ass, Carl. Okay, I can spare a guy. I'll send Tony there today. I'll have him call you if he finds out anything. Now, get to work," Mike said.

"Thanks, I'm on it," Carl said, then they both hung up.

Mike sent Tony, one of his henchmen, to join Jason's

crew, so he could try to find where the twins and Jason went. Tony, a big guy, in his early thirties, had been around the block a few times. He knew how to get information when he needed it, one way or another. When Tony walked into the office, the only ones who were there at the time were Jacob and Dave. Jacob was back in Jason's office while Dave was out front.

"I'm looking for work. Are you hiring?" Tony asked.

"We could use another hand. Here, fill this out and after we check some references and see what experiences you have, we can discuss it further," Dave said.

"I'd really like to speak with Jason," Tony said.

"You know Jason?" Dave asked.

"Yeah, we had a few beers and played pool together. Where is he?" Tony said looking around.

Dave knew all the guys that Jason hung out with, and this fellow wasn't one of them. Dave also knew that Jason had been too busy with Abby and Leo to go drinking and playing pool. This guy was full of shit, and Dave knew it.

Jacob was in the hall, and was listening while in the storage room.

"He took a little vacation. He was overdue," Dave said.

Jacob knew there was something not quite right, so he called a couple of the crewmen to come in to the office, in case there was trouble.

"Where did he go?" Tony asked.

"I'm not sure, and why do you want to know?" Dave said, now getting suspicious.

Tony pulled out a gun and put it to Dave's temple, "Because this says I have a right to know. Now start talking or I blow you away."

Jacob called the crew back and filled them in. He told them to call Coop. He knew he had to cause a distraction in order to help Dave, so he casually walked into the front holding a bunch of papers, like he needed to talk to Dave.

"Dave, how soon until the mall site is done?" Jacob said.

He tossed the papers at Tony and pushed him from the back, knocking him off balance. Tony turned and shot Jacob. Jacob went down. Dave went to jump Tony, but Tony ran out the front door. The crew ran in just in time to see Tony squeal away in a beat up truck.

"Call 911. Jacob took a hit," Dave yelled, "Hang in there, Jacob. I think he just grazed ya in the arm."

Dave ripped off his shirt and wrapped Jacob's arm to apply pressure.

"I'm okay. It hurts like hell, but I'll be okay," Jacob said.

Sheriff Cooper ran in the door. "Jacob!" he yelled. Then ran over and knelt down beside him.

"He'll be okay, Coop," said Dave, "He was lucky it was just a graze. Did you guys catch the bastard as he ran out?"

"No. He peeled out just as I pulled in. What happened here?" Coop asked as paramedics tended to Jacob.

"That guy claimed he was looking for work, but what he was really looking for was Jason. When I wouldn't give him what he wanted, he pulled a gun on me. Jacob snuck up on him and threw a bunch of papers at him, knocking him off balance. The gun went off, and you know the rest. Jacob saved my life," Dave said.

"I'm following the ambulance to the hospital. Do you want to ride with me?" Coop asked Dave.

"Yeah....yeah, I would," Dave said, and they headed out.

Tony made sure he wasn't followed then dumped the stolen truck. He called Mike.

"Mike, I need a lift," Tony said.

"What did you find out?" Mike asked.

"That Donahue's old man has quick reflexes. Other than that, nothing. The twins and Donahue split town. I had to dump the truck," Tony said.

"I'll send someone out for you," Mike said, "Then lay low for a while."

Mike hung up. He figured he might as well get the unpleasant shit done and call Carl.

"Carl, hey listen up. Tony called in. The twins and Donahue have left town. No one knows where and no one knows when they will return," Mike told him.

"Now what? I thought you said your guy was good. He couldn't even find out the whereabouts of three people," Carl replied.

"Enough Carl. Let it go for now. They will return eventually. Meanwhile, you take care of business. We will be at the North Shore tonight to pick up that shipment. I'll call you when it is done," Mike said, and hung up.

"You get that?" Sully said to the agents camped out in the van.

"I think we have all we need here. We'll send some guys to North Shore. Once the transfer is made, we'll bust them," one of the agents said.

"Hold on. Listen, Carl is getting another phone call," Sully said, and they all tune in.

After agents Reiley and Thomas followed Jason to the lodge and checked the area, they reported in that all was secure and headed back. On the drive back, after talking their usual banter, sports, Reiley commented, "Did you read that report about that Rineheart woman?"

"Most of it, why?" Thomas asked.

"Did you notice that she will be worth billions? I wonder if she even knows it?" Reiley asked.

"Probably. Wouldn't that be a nice surprise, to find out you're worth billions? I wouldn't even know what to do with all that money," Thomas said.

Reiley thought to himself, "I would". He was up to his ass in debt, and the government didn't really pay that much.

The rest of the ride back to South Carolina was quiet and uneventful. Reiley dropped Thomas back home, and started thinking again of all that money.

"That Pearlman guy is probably shitting himself not knowing where those twins are. Maybe it is time to give him a call and strike a deal," Reiley said to himself.

He pulled over and dialed Pearlman's number.

"Hello?" Carl asked, not recognizing the number on his caller I.D.

"Is this Carl Pearlman?" Reiley asked.

"Yes, who are you and what do you want?" Carl asked.

"I could be a potential client. Is that the way you always answer your phone, or are you a little strung out from losing one or two people?" Reiley said with a chuckle.

"You have my attention. Who are you and again, what do you want?" Carl asked.

Reiley could hear his impatience.

"Who I am is of no importance. What I know could be very important to you. I know where the twins are," Reiley said.

"What twins?" Carl asked.

"Now, don't be coy. The Rineheart twins," Reiley said.

After a few minutes of silence, Carl asked, "Where are they?"

"Not so fast. I am aware that you are in charge of the Rineheart estate. I need you to transfer two million into a bank account first. I'll give you the numbers. As soon as I see it is done, I'll give you the exact coordinates of their location," Reiley said.

"How can I trust you?" Carl asked.

"You can't, but what choice do you have? They are pretty well hidden. I know, I followed them. Let's just say I have government connections, and I'm sure you know that their wages aren't very high. All I want is to be able to retire comfortably. I will call you back as soon as I see the money is in my account," Reiley said, then hung up.

"What do I care about a mere two million? I will soon have billions," Carl said to himself, then proceeded to make the transfer. True to Reiley's word, he called back.

"That was quick," Reiley said.

"Give me what I paid for," Carl said.

"I'm texting it now. Oh, I know for a fact that they will be there for at least three weeks. Happy hunting, and nice doing business with you," Reiley said, then hung up.

Carl immediately made plans, and wrote up a contract

that he planned on having Abby sign. He then gathered up about six of Ianareno's goons. He told Julia that he was going on a men's retreat, and that he would be gone for a few days. He then packed and left.

Sully and the agents were still listening to the conversation. After Carl hung up Sully said, "Do you recognize that voice?"

"Fuck, that sounds like Reiley. It makes sense, his family put him in the poor house, and he was one of the agents that followed Donahue and the twins to the lodge. He would know the coordinates. I'll have to call this in," one of the agents said.

"Hey, if you guys are all right, I'm going to head to the lodge. I feel I owe that woman, after all that has happened. They might need help up there," Sully said.

"Yeah, go. We will report everything in. Agents will be sent for Carl's capture," the agent said.

Dave and Coop were still at the hospital, waiting with Louise, for the release papers for Jacob, so they could take him home. They all went in Coop's cruiser.

On the way to Jacob's house Louise asked Coop, "Do you know where my children are?"

"Yes. They are safe, and that's all I can say for now. Don't worry, Louise. I am keeping an eye out for them. As soon as Jason can, he will call you. Just rest that they are following my orders and keeping safe for now," Coop said.

Jacob knew what was happening, for the most part, and he also knew that Coop loved his son like Jason was his own. The rest of the way home was talk of what had happened, and Coop getting as much information about the guy as possible.

Chapter 24

Everyone was well rested. Jason made a big breakfast. They were eager to start their day with a boat ride. They piled into Jason's truck. The ride to the dock wasn't very far. It was a dirt road, but Jason figured the truck would come in handy on the way back with all the supplies that they would purchase. As soon as they arrived at the dock, they got out and stared at a huge boat.

"That ain't no boat, Jason, that's more of a mini yacht," Leo said.

"Wow!" the women said in unison.

Jason just smiled and said, "My dad likes his luxuries. Come on, I'll give you a tour."

"Like I said, this ain't no boat. If it was, we wouldn't need a tour," Leo said laughing.

The boat was well taken care of. The wooden deck shined. After showing them around the top deck, Jason took them below. The steps led down into the galley, which had all the modern conveniences: stove, fridge, ample cabinets and a table that could comfortably seat six people. The galley led into the living room area that had all the comforts of home, and then some. In the back of the boat were two large bedrooms, one on each side. Each bedroom had its own bathroom.

After everyone got comfortable, Jason started down river. It was a beautiful warm day and for a while, the four of them could relax a bit. Riding the river was one of Jason's favorite things. It was calming, and a person could let his mind drift. He pointed out various sights to Leo, Renee, and Abby. He could see their wide grins and bright eyes, and that alone made it all worthwhile.

He pulled into a docking area at a small town on the river that he and his dad visited often. They got out and walked around a bit; then he took them to his favorite eating establishment. After lunch, the girls wanted to go shopping at the local stores. As much as Leo and Jason really didn't get into the "shopping" thing, they didn't want the girls walking around alone. Jason and Leo followed close behind them. There was a small clothing store that the girls eagerly went into. They had a ball trying on different tops. Renee stepped into the back of the store where they sold lingerie and spotted a hot, sexy black outfit. She looked over her shoulder and noticed that the boys were outside by the door talking. She quickly made her purchase, and asked for it to be put into a non-see through bag

"What are you up to Renee?" Abby asked, smiling at her.

"Shhhh, I don't want Leo to hear you. Wait until he gets a load of this," Renee said as she opened the bag for Abby to see.

"Oh! You are so bad! I love it. Let me know how it turns out," Abby giggled at her.

"I'm sure you will hear how it turns out!" Renee said laughing.

Just then the guys came back in, "What's all the giggling about?" Jason asked.

"Girl talk," Abby said grinning.

Renee winked at Leo, and walked out the door.

Lastly, the four of them went to the supply store and loaded up on food. They picked up several DVD's to watch at night.

"Jason, help me out here. They grabbed nothing but chick flicks," Leo complained.

Jason spotted a sci-fi that they both agreed on, so everybody was happy.

"We better head back. I don't want us walking around out in the dark," Jason said.

Everyone agreed, and Jason made sure that the ride back was slow and easy. When they docked, Leo helped Jason carry everything to the truck.

"Jason, do you care if Renee and I just hung on the boat for a bit?"

Jason looked at him and grinned, "Don't rock the boat too much."

"You are an understanding man," Leo grinned back.

"When you two are done, lock up the boat. If you follow the path that goes right off the road, it will lead you back to the lodge. Just keep to the right," Jason said.

"Will do. We'll just be a few minutes. We'll see you at the lodge," Leo said.

Abby and Jason gave Renee and Leo a wave, and headed up the road. Jason looked over at Abby. She looked content and happy. He was hoping to keep her that way.

Jason pulled up to the lodge a few minutes later and Abby grabbed a couple of bags. Jason looked to the side of the lodge and noticed that the side screen was open.

"Honey, here is the key. I want to check on something. Go on in. I'll bring in the rest," Jason said, and handed Abby the keys.

With her hands full, she opened the front door, and stepped inside. She raised her head and gasped, then dropped everything on the floor. Sitting in one of the stuffed chairs, with his legs crossed, elbows on the armrests, and chin resting on his hands was Carl.
With a glaring grin he said, "Happy to see you too Abby."

Abby saw that he was flanked by two goons.

"How did you find me? What do you want?" Abby asked, trying to keep her voice calm.

"Boys, show our little lady a seat," Carl said.

The two guys ran to Abby, and pick her up by her arms. She screamed for Jason as they lifted her and placed her in a chair right in front of Carl.

"Now, now. No sense in screaming. I do believe your Jason is a little tied up right now," still grinning.

"What did you do Carl? Don't you dare hurt him!" Abby yelled.

"If you do as I say, I'll be on my way, and no one has to be hurt. I have been trying to catch up with you for a long time. You are a hard one to keep up with," Carl said, still grinning.

Back at the boat, Leo looked up at Renee and said, "I thought we could take care of some unfinished business before we head back."

"What business?" Renee asked, smiling back.

"Oh. It seems to me that a certain lady slapped my ass the other day, so she deserves a spanking," Leo said as moved toward her.

Renee turned, laughing and running to get away. Leo was right behind her. She led him on a chase around the boat's deck. He finally caught her, picked her up fireman style, and carried her below deck. She wiggled and squirmed, so he gave her ass a slap, and put her down. He sat on the couch, and laid her over his knees. He pulled her shorts and thong down giving her one cheek a firm slap. He watched his hand print appear and said, "Baby, your ass is so beautiful. This is giving me a hard on."

He noticed that she wasn't complaining, so he gave her other cheek a slap. Then he slapped both cheeks and massaged them.

"Are you okay?" he asked while lowering his head to look at her. She gave a groan and smiled up at him. "You are going to undo me woman!" he said slapping each cheek again. He then took his finger and stuck it in her pussy, "Babe, you are soaked. You do like this don't you," he said softly.

"You are the first one that has ever done this to me, and yeah, I like it. But now you are going to have to fuck me," Renee said, while rising up on his lap and placing her lips against his.

"My perfect girl, if I must, I must," he replied, while lowering her on the couch.

Leo sat up only long enough to rip off his clothes and remove hers. He grabbed a rubber out of his jeans and handed it to her.

"Here, you get to put on his hat."

"So you do know how to accessorize," she said, and ripped the packet open.

She slowly put it on his rock hard penis while smiling up at him. Leo groaned.

He grabbed his cock, and rubbed the head up and down her pussy entrance, then slid in slowly. When he was fully seated he looked into her eyes, seeing that they were glazed over, he devoured her mouth with a luscious kiss. Renee started to lower and raise her hips. Leo held her hips still.

"Baby, hold still just for a few seconds, so I can gain some control. You have me so fucking excited. I want it to last longer than a blink," he said, smiling down at her. Leaning on one arm, he reached up and grabbed one of her breasts.

"Your tits are just right. They fill my hands with a little extra. I love them."

He put his mouth on a nipple, and sucked and nibbled. Renee moaned. He then reached over to suck and nibble on the other breast.

"Leo...please....fuck me. I need you to move," she said breathlessly.

Leo rose up on both hands, raised his hips so very slowly until only the tip of his cock was in. He looked down at Renee, held on for a couple seconds, then rammed it home. Renee gasped and moaned and grabbed his ass cheeks and squeezed.

"Fuck Leo. More...oooohhh please. Harder. Faster, fuck me faster," Renee groaned.

Leo lowered onto his forearms and reared back and thrust forward. In and out, thrust after thrust. He increased his speed as sweat formed on his forehead

"Aaahh....Renee.....fuck, I'm close. Are you ready to come with me?" he asked.

She looked up at him and didn't even have breath enough to talk, so she just nodded. With her nod, he pistoned in and out until she felt him swell up inside her and that put her over and she screamed in ecstasy. Her scream sent him flying, and he held onto her as he came jetting into the rubber still fucking her. He laid on top of her and both tried to breathe air into their lungs. He looked down at her and kissed her passionately. He slowly pulled out of her. They both winced and groaned.

"Babe, as much as I would love to just lay here with you and do this again, we better head back before it gets dark," he said, and helped her up.

"I guess we should have light so we can find our way back," Renee replied.

They both dressed. After straightening up everything, Leo locked up the boat, and they started heading back.

They kept walking to the right when they heard Abby's scream for Jason. They looked at each other, and started running toward the lodge. At the edge of the woods, Leo spotted Jason on the ground, knocked out with his hands tied behind his back.

"Renee, honey, you stay right here. Don't you move until I come and get you. Do you understand?" Leo said.

"Yes, Leo please don't get hurt. Come back to me," she said, and watered up.

"I'll be back," he said, while he cupped her head and kissed her forehead.

Leo snuck around the other side of the lodge. He spotted four guys sitting on the back porch smoking cigarettes and bull shitting. He turned the other way and headed toward Jason. He reached one of the living room bay windows and slowly looked in. He couldn't believe what he saw, Carl with a gun on his lap, talking to Abby. He saw two goons on either side of Abby. He knew he had to get to Jason. He got on his belly and crawled over to him.

"Jason, come on man, you have to wake up. Jason!" he said as he slapped his face and shook him. He then untied Jason, and saw that he was starting to wake up.

"Jason, wake up. Looks like you were gun butted on the head," Leo whispered, as Jason slowly began to rise up.

"What's going on?" Jason asked, while rubbing his head.

"There are four goons in the back and two inside with Abby," Leo said.

"Do you know who they are?" Jason asked.

"That's not all. Carl is in there with them, and he has a gun," Leo said.

Jason tried to jump up but staggered. Leo grabbed his arm.

"Hold on a minute. We can't go in there half-cocked. Let's see if we can hear anything. It looked like he was just talking to her," Leo said.

They crept over to the front door that was still partly open.

"What do you want Carl?" Abby asked bitterly.

"Now is that the way to talk to your estate manager?" Carl asked.

"I know it was you behind my parents' death. How could you? Did you hate them that much? You have been behind it all haven't you?" Abby asked.

"Well, I didn't plan on Leo living after I had him kidnapped from the hospital," he said matter-of-factly.

Abby gasped, "Why Carl? My parents loved you. Leo and I did nothing to you," she asked.

"Your dad had everything handed to him. He had no idea what it was like to struggle," Carl yelled at her.
It made her jump.

"My dad was brilliant. You were jealous of him. All this is because of jealousy?" she asked softly.

"Enough. I brought a contract for you to sign. Sign it and I and my guys are out of here," he said, then handed her some papers.
She read over them and looked up at him.

"This is a release to my inheritance turning everything over to you. You killed my parents and tried to kill me and my brother for money?" she cried.

"Money that should have been for me to begin with. Now sign the damn contract," he yelled at her again.

The two guys grabbed both her arms and forced her over to the coffee table where she placed the contracts. When they grabbed her Jason jumped, but Leo stopped him and whispered, "No, not yet. Hang on."

The one thug grabbed her hand and placed a pen in it then took her arm and forced her to sign the contract. He then handed it over to Carl.

"Well, that will do. It is legible enough. Now that the hard stuff is done, say good bye Abby," he sneered and started to grab his gun.

Gunshots went off in the back of the lodge, and Carl sent his two men to go check it out, telling them that he had the situation under control.

As soon as the two guys left the room, Leo whispered to Jason, "Now."

They came in the front door running, tucking and rolling in two different directions. Carl jumped up and started shooting. Abby dove under the coffee table. More shooting was heard out back. Then there was one more shot inside the house, Abby looked up and screamed. Carl fell to the floor with a bullet in his head. Behind him stood Sully.

"Clear," Sully yelled, and agents started running in all directions, searching and yelling when each room was safe.

Jason ran over to Abby and gathered her in his arms. Leo ran outside to find Renee.

Abby looked up at Sully and said, "Thank you for saving our lives."

Sully smiled and said, "I'm sorry that things couldn't have been smoother. At least I can say this, it's over Abby. It's finally over."

"No, it is not over yet," Abby said while climbing out of Jason's lap. She went over to the coffee table, grabbed the contract and ripped it up in little pieces and said, "Now it is over."

After all the preliminaries were done and the agents got all the information that they needed, Sully pulled Jason aside and said, "You better give your dad a call. He was shot in the arm and taken to the E.R."

Jason jumped up and dialed, "Mom, how's dad? I just found out."

"He's here son. He is fine. Are all of you alright?" she asked.

"Yeah, we are fine. Can I talk to him?" Jason asked.

"Sure, here he is," Louise said, then handed the phone to Jacob.

"Hey son! How's the lodge treating you?" Jacob asked.

"How did you know? Never mind. Coop. How's the arm? What happened?" Jason asked.

"My arm is fine, it just needed some stitching up. I'll fill you in with all the rest when you get home. When are you all coming home?" Jacob inquired.

"We are going to hang here a couple days, then head home. They want me to take them on the boat again," Jacob said.

"How's she running?"

"Like a dream, dad. Like a dream. Give mom a kiss for me. I'll see you both in a couple days. I love you both," Jason said.

"We love you too son," they both said, and hung up.

Chapter 25

A couple hours later, everyone had left, and the coroner had taken Carl's body. Everyone was exhausted, and just sitting around the living room.
Jason stood and said, "I don't know about you guys, but I am sore enough to sit in that hot tub for at least an hour."

"Good call," Leo said, "While you fill it up, I'll go rustle up some snacks. Girls, you want to suit up or go raw?"

"Leo, you are so bad!" Abby said, then gave him a hug, "I'm suiting up. How about you Renee?"

"I'm not ready to go nude in front of cous here. We'll meet you at the tub," she said, and the girls headed up the steps.

Jason stopped Leo and said, "Thanks man for waking me up. You probably saved us all. I owe you."

"Remember what you said? We are family. That is what family does. You don't owe me anything," Leo said. Then he gave Jason a man hug with a pat on the back.

The four of them soaked in the tub for a couple hours while talking about the day and making plans for the next day. Jason noticed Abby getting droopy eyed. He felt tired with a slight headache from the lump on the back of his head. He got up and grabbed Abby's hand and said good night.

As soon as they entered the bedroom and Jason shut the door, he turned to Abby and placed her against the wall, kissing her firmly on the lips.

"I have been dying to do that all evening. Abby, if anything bad had happened to you, I don't think I could survive it," Jason said.

He proceeded to remove her two piece bathing suit. He took off his trunks, then picked her up, and gently laid her on the bed.

"Make love to me Jason," Abby sighed, as she

reached up to pull Jason close to her.

He kissed her again, then leaned up on his forearm. With his other hand he caressed her one breast while sucking on the other. He gave her nipple a nip and pulled on it, making her moan.

"You like that, baby, don't you," he stated.

He then started to feed on her other breast. She gathered her arms around his neck, and ran her fingers through his long, soft hair. Her hips started to rock back and forth, as his biting on her nipples sent an electric shock straight to her pussy.

She could feel his stiff cock against her belly as it throbbed. Abby took her hand and reached between them grabbing his cock, starting an up and down motion along the shaft. He groaned, releasing her nipple and continuing to kiss up her chest to her neck. He grabbed her ear lobe and gave it a tug, making her moan again.

"Jason, I need more. Please put your cock in me. I need to feel you inside me," she said, as her back arched up to receive him.

Jason moved her hand and guided his cock head up and down her clit, making them both shutter.

"Fuck me Jason. Please fuck me!" Abby yelled.

"Baby, you undo me. As soon as my cock feels that soft warm pussy, skin to skin, I lose all control," Jason said with a tense voice.

His jaw was already clenched trying to hold back.

"I'm close. Fuck me hard and fast. Don't worry about it, we can always do it again," she said, looking him in the eyes and smiling.

While looking back at her, he filled her up to the hilt and they both groaned together. He started pumping in and out, pulling his cock out to where only the tip of the head was still in, and then inch by inch reentered, until he knew each time that he hit her sweet spot. He wrapped her legs around his ass so he could go even deeper. Her breathing hitched, and they both were sweating. He pumped in and out again, slowly a few more times, hearing their bodies smack together with both of them groaning.

"Fuck Abby! Hold on baby I'm close to coming. Aaah....fuck!" Jason yelled, reared up and fucked her fast and hard, rocking their bodies into the headboard.
She arched up meeting his thrust then she let out a scream. "Jason, fuck....aaah...I'm coming."
Her body shivered and her hips bucked up. Jason rose up on his hands to thrust hard and stilled, while shooting hard into her. He gave two more thrusts each time jetting strongly into her. They both collapsed breathing hard and grasping for air. After a few minutes, as much as he didn't want to move, he pulled out of her, rolled to his side and gathered her into his arms.

In the other bedroom, Leo and Renee were in bed listening to Jason and Abby.

"Now that sounded like an adrenaline fuck," Leo said, smiling at her, "Do you need one also?"

"Bring it on, baby! I'm wet and ready to fuck," Renee said, smiling back at him.

"Can I finger fuck your ass at the same time?" Leo grinned.

"I don't know. I've never done it before. Will it hurt?" she asked.

"I've never done it either. Always wanted to, but couldn't find a willing woman. It's supposed to turn you on. Just thinking about doing it makes my dick twitch. I'll take it slow and if it hurts, you tell me and I'll stop," Leo looked at her with serious eyes.

"Okay, I'll give it a whirl," and she handed him a tube of lubricant.

"You are definitely what every man dreams of having. Get on all fours and stick that beautiful ass in the air. You are going to get fucked!" Leo said.

He flipped her around, grabbed a hunk of her long brown hair holding it like a reign and giving a snug pull, then didn't hesitate to mount her. His hands shook putting the condom on. A couple firm slaps to each cheek, a "Yee haa" and he was in and pumping.

Renee looked over her shoulder and said, “Easy there cowboy!”

Leo bent down and kissed her shoulder, and while still pumping her pussy he lubed up his fingers. He stuck one finger in her ass and slowly rubbed the lube around. Then he added two fingers, and his cock swelled as he kept pumping to a slow rhythm.

“Babe, I wish you could watch this. It is so hot. Your ass is a cherry pink and my fingers are disappearing inside you. How’s it feel?” Leo was already working up a sweat.

“Give me more. Use three fingers!” Renee hissed over her shoulder.

He stuck a third finger in her ass, and started pumping his hand at the same time as his cock was filling her up completely.

“Fuck me!.....aaahhh shit fuck! Renee you are so hot! Your pussy is gripping me like a damn vice. I’m going in fast and hard baby. Get ready to come with me,” Leo said in between breaths.

He picked up speed, rocking her body and the bed. Renee gave a garbled groan then yelled.
“Fuck!.....Me!......Leo!.......Aaaahhhh!”

Her body bucked up to meet his pistoning cock in her pussy. Leo let go right after he felt her spasm on his dick, and groaned just as loudly as she did. He pulled out of her, and flopped on the bed pulling her chest up so she could rest her head on him. She could feel his heart beating just as fast as hers.

After they caught their breath, he rubbed her back, pulled the covers up, and they fell asleep.

The next morning Leo let Renee sleep in and headed to the kitchen. Jason was there making coffee.

“I noticed that you and Renee like to play,” Jason said with a grin.

“You and Abby started it,” Leo replied.

“Yee haa cowboy?” Jason laughed.

“Are you making breakfast or am I?” Leo said, not taking the bait.

"I'll make it since you had such a wild ride last night," Jason said grinning.

"You are just jealous. Keep it up and I'll flatten you," Leo said with a smile.

"I'm done. I must say, it was entertaining. You two got our motors running again," Jason laughed.

By the time the girls came downstairs, Jason and Leo were done razzing each other. The four of them ate then headed out the door to walk to the boat.

Chapter 26

Mike tried a half a dozen times to reach Carl by cell, but it kept going to voice mail. "Where the hell is he?" Mike thought to himself, "Fuck it. We'll have to go without him."

"Come on guys. I can't reach Carl. We have to leave now or possibly miss the shipment," Mike said to his men.

"Good. That's more dope for us to test," one of the guys said with a grin.

They all plowed into two SUV's, Mike and six men, and headed to the pick-up point on the North Shore. Unknown to Mike, the F.B.I. agents were already there, in hiding, waiting for the money exchange.

"Where's my money?" the captain of the ship asked.

"You know the score. We get to check out the goods before payment," Mike answered.

"This way."

One of the ship's crewmen led the group below deck to a dark and damp room. The door opened and they entered. Mike turned on a light and told the crewman that they needed a few minutes to check things out, and he closed the door and locked it.

On the cold, metal floor sat about a dozen large boxes. One of the men took out a knife and cut one of the boxes open to reveal hard blocks of hashish. Several of the thugs took small samples and began to smoke.

"Hey, Mike, this is some damn good shit," one of them commented.

"We'll take the lot of them," Mike said, and handed the captain an envelope.

The captain opened the envelope and pulled the money out and counted it. Afterward he put it back in the envelope, pulled out a badge and said, "You are all under arrest."

The agent that posed as the captain said, "One more

thing. Your fellow partner in crime is dead."

"Who's that?" Mike asked acting tough.

"Carl," the agent said.

"That's no excuse for not returning my calls," Mike said with a grin.

"Come on wise guy. You can lead the other scum bags to the van," the agent said.

That quickly, the "crew" all produced badges, and cuffed Mike and his men. The real captain and crew were above deck already in handcuffs. Mike knew it was over.

Two F.B.I. agents went to Carl's house with a search warrant, and found the ledgers needed to connect everyone and everything. Even though they knew that Julia was involved also, there wasn't any evidence that would hold up in court. Before they left the house one of the agents sat her down and told her about Carl. Julia lost control. The agent stayed with her until she calmed down, and asked if there was anybody he could call for her. She said no, and asked them to please leave and let her grieve. When everyone left, she cried herself to sleep.

Chapter 27

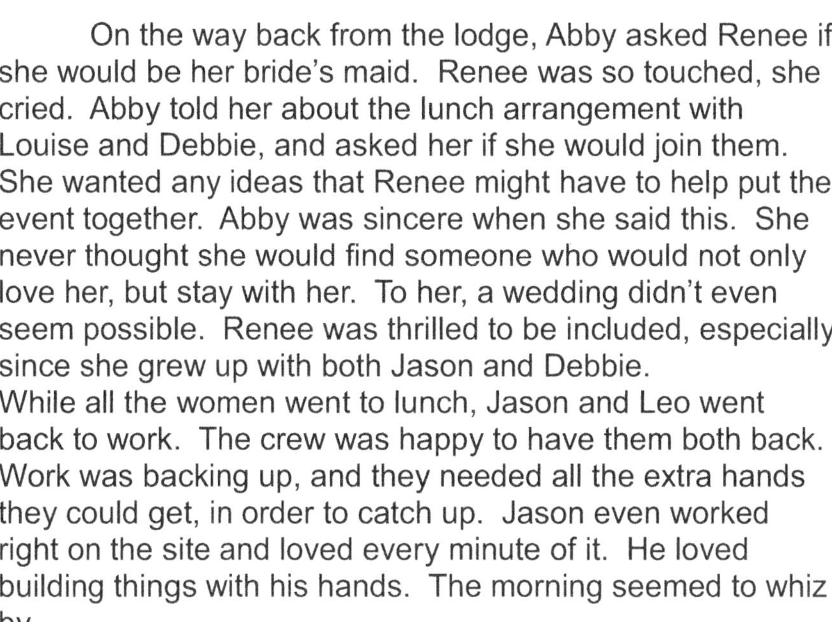

…………………♥ ♥…………………

On the way back from the lodge, Abby asked Renee if she would be her bride's maid. Renee was so touched, she cried. Abby told her about the lunch arrangement with Louise and Debbie, and asked her if she would join them. She wanted any ideas that Renee might have to help put the event together. Abby was sincere when she said this. She never thought she would find someone who would not only love her, but stay with her. To her, a wedding didn't even seem possible. Renee was thrilled to be included, especially since she grew up with both Jason and Debbie.

While all the women went to lunch, Jason and Leo went back to work. The crew was happy to have them both back. Work was backing up, and they needed all the extra hands they could get, in order to catch up. Jason even worked right on the site and loved every minute of it. He loved building things with his hands. The morning seemed to whiz by.

"Leo, let's take a lunch break. I need to ask you something," Jason said as they headed to a local diner. They sat in one of the booths in the back and placed their order. Leo looked at Jason, "What's up?"

"I need to ask you a big favor," Jason said, as he started to fiddle with his drink.

"Quit playing with your drink and just ask. What, do you want me to knock someone off?" Leo asked with a grin.

"No. Nothing that easy," Jason said, still fidgeting.

"Just spill it Jason," Leo said, getting impatient.

"Will you be my best man?" Jason said while looking him in the eyes.

Leo smiled, "You're shittin' me, right?"

"No. I mean it. If it wasn't for you, I might have never found her again. I really love your sister, and I can't think of anyone better than you to stand at our wedding," Jason said.

"I'd be honored. That means that I get to set up the bachelor party," Leo said, and wiggled his eyebrows.

"I guess you do. Try to not make it too wild. I still have to answer to Abby," Jason said, and smiled back.

The women were still at lunch in the middle of the afternoon. Abby was taken with the three women who were sitting with her. She never thought she would have a family again, and here she was with three wonderful women planning her wedding. She would agree with practically anything, because she was really doing it for them. All she wanted was to be Jason's wife. Abby could see the sparkle in Louise's eye while making the plans, and it warmed her heart.

Debbie took her duties as Maid of Honor seriously, and kept everything together.

"Mom, what do you think about the old trestle in the garage? Think dad could fix it up and paint it?" Debbie asked.

"Great idea! I could fill it with Abby's favorite flowers, and they could stand under the arch to say their vows," Louise said excitedly.

"That sounds like a lot of trouble. I don't want anybody to have to work so hard," Abby said.

"Oh, honey. Dad would love to do that. He has been driving me nuts since he retired. He loves to build things. It is right up his alley," Louise said to Abby.

"Yeah, look at it as you are doing mom a favor and getting dad out of her hair!" Debbie said, and they all laughed.

"Okay then, it sounds lovely," Abby said smiling.

They told Abby that since Jason and she picked a date that was just two months away that they better set up a time the following week to pick out a gown. All three wanted to be part of it, so Abby agreed. Lunch next week, same place, same time, then gown hunting.

Debbie kept notes and handed out assignments, after which they all headed home. Louise dropped Abby off at the office. Jason had told her that she wasn't to be left alone, and to drop her off at the office by four, and he would be there to greet her.

"There's my girl," Jason smiled, and greeted her with a firm hug and kiss, "How'd the lunch go?"

"Overwhelming and fun. You are so lucky to have such a loving family," Abby said.

"They're your family now also, or did you forget that?" he said with a grin.

"It will take some getting used to. I have been running for so many years that it is sometimes hard to grasp it all," she answered.

"Get used to it, baby, because they all love you already. The wedding is just a formality. As far as the family is concerned, you are already mine," Jason said.

"And you are mine," Abby said while hugging him back, "I would like to get some work done if it is alright with you."

"How about a couple hours? Afterwards I'll take you to dinner," he said.

"Sounds good," Abby answered, and walked to "her office".

Her office, just thinking of that made her grin. She never felt like she belonged anywhere, and now she had all this. "I wish mom and dad were still here to share in this with me," she thought to herself.

The following week, the girls got together, and went to the bridal shop. Abby agreed to let the three pick out one gown each for her to try on. They put their selections in the dressing room. Then the three of them went to the front by the three-way mirror, and sat in chairs waiting for Abby to come out with the first choice.

In the back, Abby looked at the three gowns. She already knew which one she was going to choose. She never was one to flaunt her body; she was more of the modest type. With that in mind, she decided to get Renee's choice out of the way first. It was a selection that made Abby shake her head and just smile. The dress was mid-thigh in length, made of see through white lace, form fitting with no back or sleeves. It had no veil, but it did have a small hat. Abby walked out. She looked at their faces and chuckled.

"Now, that is hot!" Renee said.

"Maybe for a strip club!" Debbie said.

"No," was all that Louise said.

Abby returned and put on dress two, which was Debbie's pick. It was cream in color, and satin all over. It had spaghetti straps, form fitting, and floor length with a flare at the ankle. It had a veil that was just chin length. Again, Abby stumbled out, having a hard time walking and not tripping.

"Oh, how elegant!" Debbie claimed.

"She'll be lucky not to trip and sprain an ankle," Renee said, while rolling her eyes.

"No," was all that Louise said.

Abby smiled as she put on Louise's pick. It was actually something that she would have picked herself. The whole gown was pure white satin and lace, with a form fitted bodice of satin, covered with lace and beading. It had long sleeves of lace that formed a point on the top of her hands. The gown filled out in layers from the waist to the ground, covered with lace and beading. The veil went to the bust in the front, and in the back it fell to the floor. She felt like a princess. She slowly walked out, with a huge smile on her face, to see what the others thought.

"Oh Abby, you look beautiful!" said Renee.

"Honey, that is definitely you," Debbie said grinning.

"That's the one for you, Abby. I knew it would be," said Louise lovingly.

Chapter 28

Several weeks had gone by, and in that time, the Ianareno family had been put through heavy scrutiny. Carl's funeral had come and gone. Abby told Jason that she needed to check on her parents' estate now that Carl was no longer guardian. Jason mentioned that his uncle, John Donahue, was an attorney, and he would gladly help her out since he took care of all legal matters concerning the family's business.

Jason took Abby to meet Uncle John, and he was more than happy to help. He took all pertinent information. They set up a time to meet the following week. Abby was nervous about the meeting, so when it was time, Jason went with her.

"Have a seat Abby; you too Jason," Uncle John said, "After reading the will, there are a couple important things we have to address before we can continue. First, upon your estate manager's untimely death, the will stated that you are now in charge of your parents' full estate."

"I'm not twenty five yet," Abby said.

"It was stipulated that if your estate manager did die, as long as you were eighteen, you were to inherit everything immediately," Uncle John said gently.

Abby looked up at Jason, "I don't know what to do?"

"Honey, Uncle John will help you. Don't worry so much. This is good news," Jason said.

"Next," Uncle John continued, "there was a clause in the will that stated that if your twin should ever be found, that your parents would hope that you would do the right thing and give him a portion of the estate. The portion to be determined by you."

"Jason, now I really don't know what to do," Abby said sounding lost.

"Abby, I may not be a billionaire, but our family is in

the millions. In all reality, I could keep you very comfortable without you even touching your estate. This is strictly your decision," Jason said, while holding her hand.

"Abby, give yourself some time. We can meet up again next week. Bring Leo with you if you decide to include him, as he will have paperwork to sign," Uncle John said.

"Of course Leo will be included, and we will be bringing him with us next week. Thank you Mr. Donahue," Abby said.

"It's Uncle John to you, Abby. You are marrying my nephew, and you are more than welcome. This is all good, so don't fret. You will do the right thing. You are a good person; you have to be or Jason wouldn't be marrying you. Oh and one more thing, welcome to the family," Uncle John said, while rising to give her a kiss on the forehead.

Abby smiled.

"Let's go home, sweetheart. Enough for one day," Jason said, and shook his uncle's hand on the way out.

When they got home, there was a note on the fridge telling them that Leo was staying at Renee's.

"Let's get naked and hit the hot tub," Abby suggested.

"You pour us some wine and make a tray of snacks, and I'll get the tub ready," Jason said.
He darted up the steps two at a time.

Twenty minutes later they were soaking and drinking wine.

"I love this tub," Abby said with a sigh, "I have so much on my mind that it is all jumbled up."

"I know, baby. It seems like it is never ending. I'll help you any way I can. All you have to do is ask," Jason said.

"What do I do about Leo?" Abby asked.

"What do you want to do? What does your heart say?" Jason asked.

"My heart says to give him half. He is half of me, and helped save my life. He actually has had it harder than me, going from foster home to foster home. I'm lucky to have him in my life," Abby said with tears in her eyes.

Jason smiled at her. He reached for her to put her back against his chest so he could hold her.

"See, you know what to do. I am so proud of you Abby. You still have the ability to make my heart swell. I love you so very much."

"I love you too my future husband," Abby said, and reached up to give him a kiss.

He hugged her close and kissed her neck. She loved being in his arms. It made her feel so very safe and loved, which she was. They spent the time talking about the wedding, her legal matters, and their future plans while feeding each other cheese and crackers and drinking wine.

"Let's go to bed so I can kiss your whole body," Jason said with lust in his eyes.

Abby smiled and rose up wiggling her ass close to his face, and he bit it. She gave a yelp and jumped out of the tub, grabbing a towel and running to the bed. Jason was right behind her.

"Wiggling that lovely ass in my face, I should spank it," Jason said, and tossed her on the bed, "but I would rather lick and kiss you all over."

"I'm all yours," Abby said, and laid with her head up by the headboard.

Jason slowly crawled onto the bed from the bottom and grabbed her foot gently kissed the arch. Placing that foot down, he grabbed the other and did the same thing. Slowly he kissed and licked up her legs until he got to her thighs. She spread her legs in anticipation. He spread her further, and got comfortable resting his chest between her legs. He kissed the inside of her thighs, and she shivered. He looked up at her and smiled, then returned to his quest. He licked the outside rim of her waxed pussy. Her breath hitched. She raised her hips trying to make contact, and he just chuckled.

"Jason, lick me....please lick me," she said, and reached for his head.

Again he licked the outer rim, slowly, taking in the smell of her arousal. Her pussy was already wet and glistened with her cream. He blew on it. She groaned. Taking his thumbs, he spread her pussy lips and took a wide sweep of her clit. Her hips jerked up again, and she moaned. Grabbing her clit with his lips, he sucked and darted his tongue in and out.

"More Jason....please. I need to come," she cried.

"You taste so good and sweet. I could lick you all night."

He smiled up at her, then proceeded to lick her pussy again. She grabbed his head and pushed him where she wanted contact. He spread her pussy lips again and made a deep and wide sweep with his tongue. He sucked and licked. Licked and sucked, over and over, until he felt her pussy lips swell, then shoved two fingers inside and finger fucked her while licking. She came with a loud scream. He rubbed her pussy gently until her climax was over. Slowly he crawled up her body until he came to her nipples. His hand cupped and fondled her one breast as he licked around the areola of the other. Both nipples hardened into nubs. His mouth took in one whole nipple, and he sucked and pulled gently as she groaned and jerked her hips up to feel his solid erection.

"I need you in me Jason," she purred.

She looked into those ice blue eyes staring at her. He kissed her. She opened to receive his tongue to battle with hers in a lustful dance. His cock throbbed against her thigh.

"You taste so good," he said with quickening breaths. He rose up and positioned his penis at her entrance. He rubbed the swelling head up and down her clit. She was soaked with arousal. Penetrating slowly, they both gave a groan.

When he was fully seated inside her, he looked into her passionate green eyes and whispered, "I love you."

Her hips automatically started to rock back and forth as he pumped her with a slow easy rhythm. He fondled her breast again at the same time, and nibbled and pulled on her nubs until they stood out. She could feel his erection swell and throb, so she started to rock faster while gasping for needed air. He met her hips with forceful thrusts and picked up speed. Rising up on his hands, he reared up and pounded into her so that their sweat and skin would smack together, exciting them both.

"I'm close Jason. Don't stop....please...more. Fuck faster!" she gasped.

Looking up at him, she could see his gritted jaw and teeth as he hissed his breath trying to hold onto control for her.

"Aaaah.....fuck baby.....come now for me....not... much...longer....I .can't..hold..out," Jason said in between thrusts, as sweat formed on his forehead.

His words pushed her over the edge with a scream. Her pussy throbbed and grasped his cock. Jason gave a guttural groan, "Fuuuck....aaaah...shit baby...aaah!" His hips were pumping so fast that the bed was hitting the wall. The smacking of flesh echoed through the room as he felt his spine tingle before his come shot up through his cock to fill her completely. He collapsed on top of her and gently kissed her neck as they both heaved to catch their breaths.

"I hope it is always this good for us both," Abby said, while running her hands through his soft long hair.

"Me, too, baby. It just keeps on getting better and better," he said, smiling at her.

"I agree. You certainly know all my buttons and how to push them," she said, grinning back.

The following week went quickly as Jason, Leo and the crew worked hard at catching up at work. Abby had just about cleaned up all the records. When Jason looked into her office, he saw her face and a neat desk. She loved working at the office, knowing that she was helping Jason and the family, her family. It made her smile.

"What are you grinning about?" Jason asked, smiling at her while leaning on the door frame staring at her.

"I'm just happy," she replied.

"You ready to go meet Uncle John? We can pick Leo up at the site on the way over," he said.

"Yeah, I'm ready. I think Leo is going to be blown over by this," she said still smiling.

Jason smiled as they walked to his truck. He knew Abby would do this. He was very proud of her. He had gotten to know her very well, probably better than anybody. He knew what a gentle and generous heart she had. They swung by and picked up Leo and drove to Uncle John's office.

On the way over, Leo kept asking what it was all about, but all Abby would say was, "You'll see."

"Hi, Uncle John," Jason said as they headed into his office.

"Hey Jason and Abby. You must be Leo, I can see the resemblance. Come. Come in and have a seat," Uncle John said, as he pointed to the chairs on the opposite side of his desk. "So, Abby, have you come to a decision?" Uncle John asked.

"Yes I have," she said, and smiled to her twin.

"What decision? What's going on, sis?" Leo asked puzzled.

"It's all good Leo. Just sit and take it all in," Jason whispered in his ear and smiled.

"What have you decided Abby?" uncle John said with a knowing smile.

"My twin is to get half," she said, smiling and watery eyed.

"Half of what sis?" Leo asked.

"Your sister has full rights to your parents' estate. In the will was a clause that stated that upon the estate manager's death, she would gain full power. Another clause stated that if you were ever found that their wishes would be for Abby to share said estate, leaving the amount up to her discretion."

Leo froze. He was obviously dumb struck.

"Young man, you are rich," Uncle John said grinning at him.

Leo slowly got up, pulled Abby up in front of him and hugged her warmly and said, "I love you sis. Are you sure?

You don't have to give me so much, I'll still love you no matter what."

"I wouldn't be alive if it weren't for you," she said sobbing.

"You saved my life too, don't forget. You gave your blood to keep me alive," he said, while bracing her head with both hands and looking directly into her eyes.

"Then we are even; which means to me that the estate should be divided even also," she said.
She kissed him on the cheek while hugging him.

Jason smiled up at both of them and said, "Uncle John, I think you have a lot of paperwork to tend to. Come on you two. Time to go celebrate. That is if us common folk can still hang with you both!"

They both rolled their eyes, and Leo punched his arm. Jason hugged them both.

"When do you need them back, Uncle John?" Jason asked.

"I'll call when I have all the legality out of the way. Meanwhile, give me a day to get accounts set up for the both of you," Uncle John said and stood leading them to the door.

"Thanks Uncle John, for everything," Abby said and planted a kiss on his cheek and Leo shook his hand saying, "Thanks a bunch, Uncle John?"

"That's right, I'm your Uncle John, as well. Jason, take them out and celebrate. I'll call you when I have everything in order," Uncle John said and shook Jason's hand and gave him a hug as well.

The ride home was quiet. Abby and Leo looked overwhelmed. Especially Leo, considering he went from poor to uber rich in a few minutes. How do you deal with that?

"So, you two, what do you want to get with your measly billons?" Jason asked.

They both looked at him wide eyed and numb.

"How about this, Leo, why don't you get yourself a vehicle so I can stop riding your sorry ass around?" Jason said jokingly, "That would be a good start."

"I can do that. I can really own my own car…or truck. Yeah, I want to do that."
Leo spoke like he was talking to Santa Claus. Jason chuckled.

"What kind of car do you want, sweetheart?" he asked Abby as he turned down the road to home.

"Why, is my ass sorry too?" she asked with a grin.

"You know better than that," Jason answered, "What car would you like to have?"

"I wouldn't mind a powder blue Mustang convertible," she said dreamily.

"Talk about a girly car! Me, I want a truck like this one," Leo said.
Jason laughed.

"How about tomorrow we go vehicle hunting?" Jason said. "That is of course if you still want to hang with us lowly millionaires."

Abby gave his arm a punch, and Leo rolled his eyes. They agreed that the next morning the three of them would go hunting for new vehicles.

The following morning the three of them went to the car dealership and made the salesman extremely happy with two sales. It would take a day or so to get their order, but they were excited with their purchases. Jason then left for work. Abby headed to her office, and Leo went out with the crew to the site.

Things settled into an everyday pattern, which was okay for Abby. She had just about caught up with all the business paperwork, and felt very good about being able to help Jason with the company.

That evening, Leo announced that he was going to move in with Renee. Jason and Abby were happy for them. Leo said that Renee was going to help him design the home that he wanted to build for the both of them. Jason let him know that he was there to help him any way he could. Abby was happy that her twin had found a mate who would make him as happy as she was.

Jason was getting busier. Since Abby had cleaned up his records, his business had doubled. Things were finally falling into place. They had picked up their vehicles and everyday life was moving on. Abby was wondering when the other shoe would fall; she wasn't used to things being so calm.

"Dave, can you move the two vehicles in front of the building?" a local asked, "The street cleaner is heading down your way."

"Sure, ask those two guys with the red shirts over there. They won't mind. The truck belongs to Leo, and the car belongs to Abby," Dave said.

The two workers grabbed the keys and headed out to move the car and truck. They each started the engines, and then the building shook. Jason, Abby, Leo and Dave ran outside to see their crewmen blown apart along with the car and truck. The four of them just stood in utter shock, frozen in one spot.

Sirens filled the air as ambulances, fire trucks, and police cars surrounded the area. Smoke filled the air and shattered vehicle parts littered the streets. Sheriff Cooper pulled up, jumped out of his cruiser and walked up to the four of them.

"Jason, what the hell happened?" Coop said, facing the four of them.

No response from any of them.

"Jason! Jason, snap out of it! What can you tell me?" Coop said, again.

"I don't know. The building shook and I ran out here," Jason said.

"Dave, what can you tell me?" Coop asked him next.

"Ahh, I…I'm…our guys are dead," Dave said, still quite numb.

"What do you know, Dave?" Coop tried again.

"One of the city guys came in and asked if I could get someone to move Abby and Leo's vehicles. I sent the two new guys. Now they are dead."

Dave was visibly shaken.

"Jason, I need to see your security camera's recordings," Coop said.

He took Jason by the arm, leading him inside.

Leo and Abby were still standing outside, looking at all the rubble. It occurred to both of them that, if they had moved their vehicles themselves, they wouldn't be standing there now. Leo slowly grabbed Abby's hand.

"Abby, Leo, come inside with us," Coop said.

They all went into Jason's back office. Jason held Abby in his arms to stop her from shaking. Dave rewound the video to the cameras. After viewing the footage, it showed a man reaching under both Abby's car and Leo's truck.

"Anyone recognize this guy?" Coop asked.

No one recognized him. Coop took a copy of the recording, and told Jason that he would view it again at the station to see if any of his men could recognize the man. In the meantime, he advised that Jason close shop, and everyone go home. Jason had Dave notify the crew to go home after their shift, and to take the next day off. Coop asked for the new employees' information. He told Jason that he would send his deputy to their homes to inform the relatives.

In the days that followed, arrangements were made for the two crewmen's funerals. Everyone attended. It was so surreal to all of them. Abby and Leo thought that all the violence was over when Carl was shot. Now they felt like it would never end.

A couple of days passed, and in that time things settled a bit. Still, there hadn't been any identification of the man in the video. Abby didn't go anywhere alone and stuck pretty close to Jason, which is exactly what he told her to do. Leo spent just about every night at Renee's place, and Renee dropped him off at the office on her way to work. There were only a few more weeks until the wedding, and Abby was getting quite anxious. She wished she had accepted Jason's offer to go to Las Vegas to get married. Her fear was that of an attack being made on their wedding day. She hadn't mentioned her concerns to Jason; she felt he had enough on his mind.

Heading into the office, Jason kept looking over at her. Her face was covered with worry.

"What's up, babe?" he asked, "Something has you worried. It seems you get quieter the closer the wedding gets. Are you having second thoughts? Cold feet?"

"About marrying you? Never! Maybe we should just go to Vegas like you suggested," she replied, grabbing his hand as it rested on her leg.

"Where did this come from? I thought you said that you wanted a wedding for the family," Jason asked surprised.

"Jason, what if an attempt on me or Leo happens on our wedding day?" Abby asked, while looking up at him.

"Is that what has you all tied up in a knot?" he asked.

Abby just nodded her head and gave him the doe eyes she has when worried about something.

"Ah sweetheart, why didn't you tell me that that is what's been worrying you? Listen to me, no one, and I mean no one will be able to get on my dad's property without us knowing it. Coop has already offered to set up security, and he will have the place covered. Stop worrying about that and, instead, start looking forward to our day and the surprise honeymoon I have planned for us," Jason smiled at her.

"No clues, huh?" she asked.

"I'll give you one. Bring a bathing suit. Other than that, that is all the wardrobe you'll need, because I am planning on keeping you naked most of the time," Jason grinned and wiggled his eyebrows.

She smiled back and looked a lot happier.

Chapter 29

They entered the office to find Dave already there going over blueprints.

"Mornin' you two. I made coffee and, Abby, there is a stack of mail waiting on your desk. Lucky you; you get to pay bills," Dave said, and returned to his work.

Abby and Jason grabbed a cup of coffee and headed to their desks. Abby sat down. Taking a sip from her cup, she started sorting the mail. She came across an average white envelope with a stamp but no return address. It was addressed to her personally. She set down her cup slowly and opened the envelope, pulling out a single sheet of paper. It read, "You and your twin must pay for what you have done." Abby gasped. Jason jumped up and went to her.

"Let me see that, honey," Jason said taking it out of her hand.

He looked at it and with gritted teeth, cursed. Abby just stared straight ahead at nothing in particular. Jason took the paper. He had Dave call the crew to have someone bring Leo to the office. He next called Coop and told him about the note. Coop told him he'd be right there.

"I'm not running anymore, Jason. Whoever this is, I have to face them or I'll be looking over my shoulder the rest of my life. Leo will too. This is going to stop, now," she told him.

After reading the letter, Coop said he would have it analyzed, but he doubted anything would come of it. Leo agreed with Abby that they should hold their ground and be more diligent with their surroundings.

"Abby, who would have something against you? Maybe someone your parents might have known?" Coop asked.

"The only one that I was aware of is dead. That was Carl," Abby said.

"Leo, what about you?" Coop turned and looked at him.

"I have been on the move all my life. I haven't stayed in one place long enough, until now," Leo answered.

"Any luck with the video?" Jason asked.

"One of my guys said that the man looked like one of Ianareno's goons, but he couldn't be positive. We are still working on that. Keep safe you two, and I'll be in touch if anything comes up," Coop said, and walked out the door.

"I'm going back to work. I doubt anyone would try something in broad daylight with the whole crew around," Leo said, then gave his sister a kiss and left.

"Come on, Abby. The boss is taking you to lunch," Jason said, giving her a hug and kiss.

That evening, Renee picked up Leo at the site on her way to the bank. She had to go back to work for a couple hours, so she dropped Leo at her place, where he could take a shower and start something for dinner.

Abby and Jason were watching a television program when Abby jumped and looked at Jason.

"Something is wrong with Leo. Can we go over to Renee's? Just for a minute, I need to check and see that he is alright."

"Sure baby, let me grab my keys," Jason said, and they headed out the door.

It only took twenty minutes to get there. Renee's car wasn't in the driveway, and the front door was unlocked. Abby walked in with Jason right behind her. She looked into the living room and screamed "Leo!"

Leo was tied to a chair, unconscious, with blood dripping down his head. Abby ran to him and Jason checked for a pulse.

"He's alive, Abby. He's just unconscious. Untie him; then call 911 while I search the rest of the house," Jason said, and quietly stepped into the next room.

As soon as he left, a figure in black lunged at Abby screaming, "You just won't die will you!"

Abby screamed for Jason while fighting back. The attacker had her pinned to the ground with a knife ready to plunge into her when Jason banged the person on the head with a baseball bat. The attacker dropped cold. Jason turned the person over and pulled up the mask.
Abby gasped, "Julia!"

By the time the ambulance arrived, Leo regained consciousness, but with a whopping headache. He seemed to be fine, otherwise. Jason had tied Julia up so that when she woke up, she would be ready to go with Coop.

Jason looked at Abby and said, "How did you know?"

Both Leo and Abby answered at the same time, "It's a twin thing."

Julia finally admitted to hiring one of the Ianareno boys to blow up Abby and Leo's vehicles. She admitted that the twins were supposed to die, not the two men that moved the car and truck. Julia said that they deserved to die for getting Carl shot. His death had obviously put her over the edge into insanity. She would probably be committed into a psychiatric ward for a long, long time.

"Now, it is finally over," Abby said to Jason, "I can concentrate on our wedding without fear."

"I think my sister has everything in order. All you have to do is walk down the aisle," Jason said lovingly.

"Is it okay for the best man to also walk the bride down the aisle?" Abby asked.

"Why not? It is your day. You can have it any way you want," Jason smiled and hugged her.

Chapter 30

They still had a couple weeks until the wedding. Leo and Abby wanted to break away with Jason and Renee for a week in the Pocono Mountains, their treat. One of their parents' properties was there, and since they had to check out all the estates before deciding which ones to sell, they figured that the one in the Poconos would be a good place to start.

The private log cabin was nestled in the forest by Bushkill Falls, in the Pocono Mountains. Bushkill Falls is also known as the "Niagara of Pennsylvania" and is surrounded by eight scenic waterfalls. There are many hiking trails and bridges to explore, so the four of them could hike a new area every day while they were there.

Abby had finally gotten herself a good camera, complete with extra lens and case. She appointed herself the official photographer of the trip. Her love of photography showed in her natural ability of getting the right shot. Jason suggested that she open her own gallery someday.

The log cabin was huge and fully furnished. Abby knew that her parents would slip away on many a weekend and leave her with the Pearlmans. After seeing the place for the first time, she understood why they did it. The place was breathtaking, all natural wooden floors, fireplaces in just about every room, and a modern equipped eat-in kitchen. The living room had a cathedral ceiling, which made it appear even bigger than it was. There were four bedrooms upstairs, and each had its own bathroom. Outside, in back, there was a deck with a large hot tub that faced the mountains.

"I think we'll keep this place, sis. What do you think?" Leo said, while taking in the mountain side.

"It's definitely a keeper. I suggest that the men get this tub set up while Renee and I gather the food and drink.

Everyone on board with that?" Abby said, grinning ear to ear.

"You heard the lady, get in the kitchen woman, and fetch me a sandwich," Leo said, jokingly, while swatting Renee's ass.

"Woman! Sandwich! Fetch? Aren't we feeling our oats?" Renee said, smiling at Leo.

Leo grabbed her in his arms and swung her in a circle, "I'm so happy, babe. Look at this place! Someday we might bring our kids up here. I see the four of us sharing our lives up here."

"Kids? Are you saying what I think you are saying?" Renee asked.

Leo pulled something out of his pocket, went on one knee and looked up at Renee with love in his eyes. Holding up a two karat diamond ring, he said, "Renee, will you marry me?"

Renee, Jason, and Abby gasped. It was so totally unexpected!

Renee looked down at Leo, with tears in her eyes and said, "Yes, I'll marry you. But I still won't fetch you a sandwich!"

All four of them laughed and hugged each other. Abby watched her twin lovingly as he picked Renee up, again, and kissed her passionately. It had dawned on her how far the two of them had come in such a short time. It hadn't been easy, but they had been blessed.

While she was looking at them, Jason slipped his arm around her and asked, "You okay sweetheart?"

"Yeah, just reflecting," she said.

"You look so happy," he said softly.

"I am Jason. I feel so lucky to have found you, and to think it started with a glass of my homemade iced tea," she answered, looking up at him.

Jason kissed her then said, "Leo, let's get this tub going. We have a lot to celebrate!"

The evening was light and joyous. Renee kept doing things so that she could hold her hand up to flash everyone her diamond. Abby was so happy for Leo. She felt he really deserved some joy, especially with such a rough beginning.

It amazed her how well rounded he ended up, with not having anything or anyone stable in his life. Leo had a good outlook and had a gentle soul, and she was proud of him.

It was starting to get dark and chilly, although the tub still gave off steam. Leo stood up first and pulled Renee up with him.

"Come on wife to be. Let's go play," he said.

They said goodnight, leaving Jason and Abby to have some quiet time. Jason wanted Abby to soak more to ease the sore muscles and bruises that she still had from the fight with Julia

Leo chased Renee up the steps, with her giggling all the way to the bedroom. Once the bedroom door was shut, she turned and locked lips with Leo.

"If you can give me a couple minutes, I packed something special for you," Renee said softly.

"Take your time, babe, we have all night," Leo said. He brushed strands of her hair behind her ear. He loved to touch and smell her hair. It was soft as silk and smelled like vanilla.

A few minutes later, Renee sauntered in wearing black stilettos and black stockings with a black garter belt that had a little rosette in the center. Underneath, she had a black lace thong that just covered her newly waxed pussy. She wore a matching black lace bra that had the nipples exposed. It also had a little rosette in the center. With her dark straight hair, that waved around one nipple and flowed down to the center of her back, her skin looked alabaster and soft. Leo drooled, immediately going erect.

"Oh babe, just let me look at you for a few minutes. Would you mind just turning around and letting me see your gorgeous ass?" Leo said, jerking his swim trunks off.

Renee turned, then bent over and put her hands on her knees.

"Renee, if I even touch my dick, I'm going to come," Leo announced.

He went over to her and kissed each ass cheek. Then he licked each cheek, and she sighed.

"I have to spank that ass, just enough to give it a rosy glow," Leo growled.

He then spanked one cheek then the other, repeating in quick succession until her ass glowed. Renee moaned. He lovingly rubbed and squeezed her cheeks, while grinding his cock against her crack.

"Get on the bed, babe, on all fours. I'm going to fuck that sweet ass of yours and make you come," Leo whispered in her ear.

Renee could feel her pussy juices dripping down her thigh. She gracefully climbed on the bed to her hands and knees, then arching her back.

She looked over one shoulder at him and said, "Fuck me."

Climbing between her legs, with a tube of lube in his hand, he stuck a finger in her pussy.

"Shit! You are drenched!" he said.

He proceeded to stick two fingers in, rubbing her clit. Her hips begun to buck.

"Aah...Leo...hurry....Fuck my ass!" Renee groaned.

She turned to look at him as he raised his fingers to his mouth to lick off her essence.

"So sweet! I love how you taste," he said.

His cock swelled and throbbed, anxious to fuck her ass. He lubed up two fingers and slowly stuck them in her ass and finger fucked her, while using his other hand to rub her clit. Her back arched and she pushed back to take in his fingers all the way.

"Please Leo....give me your cock....stick it in my ass," she panted, dropping her head and arms down so her ass stuck up open to him.

"Rub your clit baby. I'm coming in," Leo hissed with clenched teeth.

He positioned his swollen cock head to her ass and watched as it slowly disappeared inside her.

"Fuck!....aah shit....I'll be lucky to get a couple pumps in. You are so fucking hot...tight. Push back, babe....relax. Let me in all the way," he panted.

She pushed back and he drove in, feeling his balls hit her pussy. He pulled back one inch at a time until just the tip of his cock was in, then took it back in slowly. She pushed back to him.

"It feels so good, Leo. I'm close! Take me over. Fuck faster....harder....Now Leo....oooh...now!" Renee screamed, as she climaxed hard.

Leo reared back and thrust forward. Grabbing her hips to keep her steady, he pistoned in and out of her ass, feeling the ripple of her orgasm. He looked down at his dick going in and out of her, and it made his cock swell even more.

"Aaahhhh.....fuck!....I'm coming.....shit....I can't hold on anymore...Fuuuck!" he yelled, as his eyes rolled back in his head, and he felt the slapping of his balls hit her pussy.

He stilled as his sperm shot, filling her ass, then two more quick thrusts as her ass clenched him, milking him dry. They both collapsed on the bed. For a few minutes, neither one moved, as they caught their breath.

"I take it that this means you like my outfit," Renee said in between breaths.

"That's putting it mildly," he replied, and softly kissed her neck.

He then got up and gave her ass cheek a pat, and went into the bathroom to get a warm cloth and towel. He gently cleaned her up.

"How about keeping it on a little longer. I want to play with your tits. I'm sorry I neglected them. I was overwhelmed with your sweet ass."

She rolled over. He laid next to her and gathered her in his arms.

"Although I do need a little rest first.....and maybe some food. You kind of wore me out."

"Like you said, we have all night," she said, looking up at him and kissing his jaw.

The next day, the four of them decided to pack a lunch and hit the trails. The weather was sunny, and the flowers were in bloom. Leo printed out a map of the network of trails in the area that he found on the internet. They chose the one that would show them the most waterfalls and bridges. The area was breathtaking. The natural falls were picturesque. Abby took pictures of everything, especially of the four of them. She was planning on making an album for both her and Jason and one for Renee and Leo.

The more Abby and Leo were around each other, the more it seemed to her that, in a way, they have always been connected. She had really grown to love her twin, and she knew he loved her. As the four of them were sitting by one of the waterfalls, having their picnic lunch, Abby looked at Leo and smiled. He smiled back.

"What's up sis?" he asked.

"Will you do me a favor?" she asked.

"Honey, you know that all you have to do is ask, and I'll do my best," Leo said affectionately.

"Will you walk me down the aisle?" she asked.

Renee and Jason grinned.

"I would be honored sis!" he said grinning ear to ear.

He got up and gave her a hug and kissed her on the cheek.

"You are going to be one busy guy that day, Leo," Renee said, "with having to keep my cousin in line AND walk your sister down the aisle!"

"Nothing that I can't handle. I can't wait to see the two of them finally hitch up," Leo said, and gave Jason a punch in the arm.

"Speaking of which," Jason said, "we better head back tomorrow. Debbie is all beside herself about Abby being so far away. Abby, she needs you to call her about the final fitting? Well, that's what she told me to tell you."

"I'll call her as soon as we get back," Abby said.

They packed their gear and headed back to the cabin, stopping along the way to take in the sights, or for Abby to take pictures. All morning Abby had an upset stomach, but didn't want to worry Jason. For some reason she was getting nauseous again, and had to sit down. Jason set her down on a boulder that was close to the path.

"Honey, what's wrong? You look a little green around the gills," Jason said, kneeling down in front of her. He felt her forehead, "You feel a little clammy."

"I think I ate something bad. I felt sick this morning, but just ignored it," Abby said.

"Here, eat some soda crackers. I have some in the pack," Renee said.

She pulled some out of the pack that Leo was carrying. They all sat while Abby munched on a few crackers. After sitting a while, she felt better. They made sure not to make any more detours, and headed straight for the cabin. The crackers helped, but Abby was glad when they finally made it back. As soon as they put away everything, Abby gave Debbie a call. She let her know that they would be back by the following evening. The fitting was scheduled for the day after.

The next morning, Abby was still feeling sick, so they all thought the sooner they got home the better. Jason was afraid that Abby was coming down with something, but Renee was thinking something else. She wouldn't say anything until they got home.

Chapter 31

The ten hour ride home was long, having to make additional stops for Abby to settle her stomach. She felt for the other three, because they were so worried about her. When they got close to home, Renee asked if they would please stop at a drug store so she could run in for a minute. Renee and Leo went to Jason's house with them. Renee wanted to help take care of Abby.

As soon as they walked into the house, Renee grabbed Abby's hand and said, "Come with me."

They hurried upstairs to the bathroom, and Renee pulled out a pregnancy test.

"Here, I think this is why you are sick," Renee said, handing her the test.

"No way! The doctor said I couldn't get pregnant until I started getting my period again," Abby said.

"Humor me. Take the test so at least we can rule it out," Renee said, smiling at her.

Abby opened the box and handed Renee the directions. She didn't even want to read it. What if she was pregnant? Would Jason be okay with that? Would he want to cancel the wedding?

Renee handed her the test strip and said, "Here, hold it on one end and pee on it."

Abby did as she said, then set the strip on the counter as Renee timed it. They both waited, staring at the strip. It started turning blue and a little plus sign appeared.

Renee looked at her with a huge smile and said, "Just as I thought. You two are pregnant!"

Abby just stood frozen, "How?" was all she said.

"I'm not surprised with all that hootin' and hollerin' I hear from you two every time you get behind closed doors. Abby, this is a good thing. Jason loves kids. You going to tell him?" Renee asked.

Just then there was a rapping on the bedroom door, "What's going on in there? Are you two alright?" Jason asked.

"Tell him Abby," Renee said softly, and opened the door, "I'll leave you two alone."

She hopped down the stairs with a big smile on her face.

Jason went into the bathroom, and saw Abby leaning with her back against the counter. Her eyes were huge, and he couldn't figure out why.

"Sweetheart, what's wrong?" he asked as he approached her.

"Nothing, I hope," she said.

She backed away from the counter and pointed to the strip. Jason looked down at it.

"Is this what I think it is? Are we having a baby?" he asked, with a smile slowly forming on his face.

Relief hit her as she saw his face light up. She just nodded yes.

"Oh…My….God! I'm going to be a daddy!" he yelled.

He picked her up and whirled her around once, then gently set her down. He kissed her face all over and hugged her warmly.

"We are going to have a baby! I love you so much!"

They heard Leo running up the stairs. He barged into the bathroom.

"Is it true?"

"You are going to be an uncle!" Jason said, and he gave Leo a man hug with a pound on the back.

They both looked at Abby. She had tears running down her cheeks with a big grin on her face. The two men she loved the most were there to witness this, and they both were ecstatic. She couldn't have been happier.

The four of them went into the kitchen. Renee gave the guys a beer and she gave Abby a glass of milk. Excitement filled the air. More than ever, Abby wished her mom was still alive to be with her now. She sat quietly, still a little numb, while the other three rattled on about the baby.

Jason and Abby both agreed to wait until after the wedding to let the rest of the family in on the news. The wedding itself was enough excitement for everybody. When they got back from the honeymoon, they would tell Jason's parents, first. Renee and Leo promised that they wouldn't tell a soul.

Renee helped Abby set up a doctor's appointment, and gave her some tips on how to keep the morning sickness at bay. Leo and Renee said good night and headed to Renee's house. The girls had to get some sleep in order to get to the morning appointment for the final fitting.

The fitting appointment went well. No adjustments were needed for anyone. Although, Renee looked like the cat that ate the canary. Every time she looked at Abby, the both of them broke out in a huge grin. Debbie and Louise couldn't figure out what the two of them were up to. After the appointment, the four girls drove to the local diner for lunch.

"Okay, spill it Renee. What are you two up to?" Debbie asked.

"Oh nothing. Jason won't tell Abby where he is taking her for their honeymoon, and I have a pretty good idea where," she answered to cover up their secret.

"How would you know?" Debbie asked.

"I have my ways. That's all I'm saying. So, how are the kids?" Renee asked. She knew that both Louise and Debbie loved to talk about her two kids. Debbie rattled on about how her daughter, Alice Louise, kept running around with the basket that she would carry down the aisle. Rose petals would probably be thrown everywhere. They all laughed. Louise mentioned how she had been working with her grandson, Little Jacob, in teaching him how to hold a pillow up and walk at the same time. Abby smiled, visualizing how cute the two of them would be.

Just as Renee figured, Debbie and Louise forgot about her and Abby smiling at each other. They talked about plans for the wedding and finalizing things. The day before the wedding, they were all to meet at Jason's mom's house for the rehearsal dinner. Kisses and hugs were passed around, and everyone left for home. Renee took Abby to the office to meet Jason.

At the office, Abby heard laughter coming from the break room, so she headed there to find Leo and Dave talking about something by the coffee machine. She gave Leo a questioning look.

"Hi sis! How'd lunch go?" Leo said, and walked over to her, "Talk later, Dave."

"Yeah, I'll get right on that thing, ah, by now," Dave replied, acting awkwardly.

"You didn't tell him did you?" Abby asked in a whisper.

"No, of course not. It's not my place," Leo said. He gave her a kiss on the forehead. "How are you feeling?"

"Okay, under the circumstances. What was that all about?" she asked pointing to Dave as he stepped out the doorway.

"We are planning a bachelor party for Jason. You can't say anything; he thinks I forgot about it," Leo said grinning.

"Are there going to be strippers?" Abby asked in a serious way.

"I sure hope so," Leo said, "Sweetheart, Jason has eyes for only you. You should know that by now. We just want to have a good time watching him squirm."

"You're evil," she said, grinning back at him, "Mum's the word."

Jason walked in then and went to the coffee machine. "How'd the luncheon with the ladies go?"

"It went very well. Renee almost gave it away with her grinning at me every time I made eye contact with her," Abby said smiling, while giving Jason a hug.

"Debbie is one sharp cookie. She probably caught that," Jason replied, pouring himself a coffee.

"She did. Renee said she knew where you were taking me for our honeymoon for her cover," Abby said looking up at him, "Does she know?"

"No, but that was a good cover," Jason said, knowing that she was fishing for clues, "Are you going to do any work or just hang around the break room until it is time to go home?"

"I'm heading to my desk, boss!" Abby said then stuck her tongue out at him, "Oh, and good cover yourself."

Jason chuckled and gave her a swat on the ass as she sashayed to her office.

After a few hours of work, Abby and Jason headed toward the front door to quit for the night. Dave was still doing something at the front desk.

"Working late?" Jason asked.

"I just want to work on the schedule a little before heading out. You two have a good evening," Dave looked up and waved.

As soon as they shut the door, Dave called Leo, "They just left. It's a go!"

Leo headed to the office, and Dave started making the necessary phone calls. As the crew and family males started heading in, each bringing either booze or food, Leo told everyone to hide back in Jason's office. It was the biggest room, and he didn't want Jason to see anyone until he got back there. When everyone was situated, Dave gave Jason a call.

"Jason, I hate to bother you, but you better get back down here. There is this city ordinance person here stating that she has to shut down the office due to some tax you didn't pay," Dave said in a serious tone.

"What the fuck is she talking about?" Jason answered, pissed off.

"You got me. She said that she has to talk directly to you, or she will bar the front door. You better get down here, now!" Dave said.

"Alright, alright. I'll be right there," Jason said, and hung up.

"Okay everyone. Places. He'll be here in ten minutes. Here sweetheart, you get to sit on top of the desk," Dave said, as the stripper, done up in a skimpy leather outfit, complete with a whip, giggled

Dave went out to wait for Jason. Jason came storming in the door in a huff.

"Where the fuck is this person?"

"I had her go to your office and wait," Dave said, keeping a very serious face.

Jason stormed down the hall and opened his office door to see a scantily dressed, big-titted woman, with no bra, crack her whip saying, "Come here you bad boy. You need to be punished for not paying your sex tax!"

All the men yelled "OOOOUUUW Jason. That is sooo bad!"

Then music started, and so did all the hooting and laughing. Jason stood at the doorway and looked around, seeing all his male friends and family as they circled around him.

"You thought I forgot, didn't you?" Leo said, proud of himself.

"Just wait until it is your turn!" Jason said, relieved and breaking out into a huge grin.

The stripper had Jason take a seat, front and center and did a strip tease and lap dance that made him sweat. It made them all sweat!

Afterward, he said out loud, "Abby better not find out about any of this!"

They all laughed and reassured him there is a bachelor party code that cannot be broken, "What happens here stays here!"

The stripper ended up giving every guy that wanted a lap dance, a really good one. Jacob and Coop sat off to the side keeping an eye on things, so they didn't get too rowdy. Jason went over to them and shook their hands.

His dad smiled and said, "You should have seen the look on your face, son. It was priceless!" and he and Coop laughed.

"Yeah, Leo got me good, but his turn will be coming next," Jason said to both of them, "He asked Renee to marry him, and she said yes."

"No shit! He's a good guy. I'm happy for the both of them. God knows, Renee deserves some happiness," Jacob said.

"I couldn't agree more. Leo will take good care of her; he is nuts over her," Jason said.

The three of them looked over at Leo filling everyone's drink and passing out food.

"Dad, will you do me a favor?" Jason asked, looking seriously at him.

"Sure, son. What do you need?" Jacob asked.

"Will you stand with me and be my groom's man?" Jason said smiling.

"Took you long enough to ask! I was afraid you wouldn't. That is something that I have always wanted to do, stand with my son as he got married," Jacob said with a grin.

Jacob actually looked relieved and the joy showed in his face. "You're girl is one tough little lady, Jason. We love her, your mom and I. We couldn't be happier for you. Not to mention that I haven't seen the books for the business in better shape than since she had tackled them. I know you will take good care of her. I'm proud of you, son," Jacob said and gave him a hug. He looked around at everyone having a good time and said, "Boy, they are really trashing the place, aren't they?"

"That's one of the reasons that us two are here, Jason. We volunteered to be the cleanup committee. No worries, go have a good time," Coup said.

Jason smiled and thanked them both. They drank and ate and had one hell of a good time. Leo tipped the dancer extremely well before she left. Each guy that got a lap dance tipped her. She probably made over a thousand dollars. Not bad for a few hours work

Leo didn't drink. Being best man, he had to make sure that Jason got home safe and sound. He dropped him off around three in the morning. Abby tried to wait up for him, but ended up falling asleep on the couch.

"Look at her, Leo. God love her, she tried to wait up for me. I hope you called her to let her know what was going on," he asked.

"Of course. I would never worry her like that. She knew all about it," Leo said.

"Even the stripper?" Jason asked, a little concerned.

"Even the stripper. I left out all the details, so, use discretion," Leo said laughing.

"Thanks Leo. I never suspected a thing. I had a blast, and I know everyone else did also. I knew I did the right thing picking you as best man," he said, as they did a fist bump, "I better carry her up and get her to bed. I'll see you at the rehearsal dinner?"

"I wouldn't miss it," Leo said, and left.

Chapter 32

The rehearsal went off without a hitch. Everyone knew what they had to do and where they had to stand. The dinner was at Jason's parents' house and everyone chipped in. The mood was festive with a lot of laughter. Jason and Abby looked at each other and smiled. They both knew in a few hours, it would be official. Jacob and Louise sent everyone home early, so there would be no excuses for being late in the morning.

"You're with me tonight, Abby," Debbie said, "You'll have to suffer tonight big brother. You can't see her now until you see her walking down the aisle. So say your good nights, and let's get this thing going!"

Jason grabbed her, pulled her up against his chest and dipped her low into a full lip lock, complete with tongue, while everyone hooted, hollered, and oooohhhhed! His kiss made her dizzy, and she almost fell, but he caught her.

"Thanks," Abby said, smiling with her swollen lips.

"I'll always be there to catch you babe," Jason said.

"Let's go. Enough of the mush," Debbie said smiling She grabbed Abby's arm. They both waved to everyone as they headed out the door.

"Why don't you boys stay here tonight? Your tux's are here anyways. That way we can all leave together," Louise said to Jason and Leo.

"Yeah, we can keep him from running," Leo said to Jacob, laughing.

"The only place I'm going is to bed. I doubt I'll sleep though. Thanks Mom, it will feel strange sleeping in my old room, but I think you are right. I don't want any of us to be late,"

Jason stood, gave his mom a kiss then went upstairs to his old room. Louise showed Leo to the spare room, and told him to just holler if he needed anything.

Jason was the first one up the following morning. He was lucky if he slept two hours. In the kitchen he started the coffee, then sat at the kitchen table. He pulled his cell phone out of his pocket and thought, "I may not be allowed to see her, but no one said I couldn't call her." He dialed her cell and it rang just once.

"Hello?" Abby said softly.

"Good morning my bride to be," Jason whispered back, "How did you sleep?"

"Hardly at all. You will probably run away when you see the bags under my eyes," Abby said chuckling.

"Sweetheart, even at your worst, you are beautiful. I didn't think that I would miss you as bad as I did last night. I kept reaching out, and you weren't there. Sleep is overrated anyways," Jason said.

"Is that my brother? Tell him good bye, we have work to do," Debbie shouted out at Abby.

"You didn't warn me what a slave driver your sister was," Abby said, "I guess I'll see you soon. I love you, Jason."

"Ah, sweetheart, I love you too. Tell my sister she has a big mouth!" Jason said chuckling, and hung up.

Just hearing Abby's voice made him feel better. It had dawned on him that this was the first time that they hadn't slept together since she was kidnapped. It would be the last time.

After Louise made breakfast, she got everyone into the full swing of setting up the back yard. Jacob got the arch that he fixed and painted. He set it up where Louise had ordered. She had placed roses all through the lattice. They both looked at it proudly. The couple would look beautiful under it for the vows and pictures. Jason and Leo set up chairs and helped with the tables and coverings. An aisle was made between the chairs. The tables were set up on either side of the yard. Louise had made flower arrangements for each table, and ribbon laced the aisle chairs. Even though it was simply done, the back yard looked lovely. It really looked like it was ready for a wedding.

"Nice job, mom! It is more than I expected. Abby will love it," Jason said, while hugging his mother.

The caterers arrived, the cake was set up, and the guys put on their tuxes. Friends and relatives arrived and took their seats. The minister took his place at the center of the arch, and Jason and his dad took their spots.

Music started to play as Jason's little niece walked down the aisle with her basket full of rose petals. She scattered them everywhere. Everyone smiled. Next was his nephew, who proudly carried the pillow down the aisle with Jason's mom's help. The kids did a terrific job. Jason was proud of them. Next came Renee. She looked great in her powder blue chiffon gown. She winked at Jason as she passed. Debbie followed in a royal blue chiffon gown, and she stuck her tongue out at Jason and made him laugh.

There was a pause in the music. Everyone stood and turned. The bridal march started to play. Jason held his breath and looked for Abby. It seemed like twenty minutes went by, but it was only a couple. Through the sliding glass doors, leading to the yard, Leo and Abby appeared. Jason let out his breath, made eye contact with Abby and smiled broadly at her. His eyes watered up as he watched Leo help her walk to him. He thought to himself, "How did I get so lucky to get her. She is the most beautiful woman that I have ever met."

Before Leo handed her over to Jason, he lifted her veil enough to kiss her cheek and said, "Be happy sis, you deserve to be. I love you."

Tears ran down her cheeks. Jason grasped her arm firmly and held her by his side.

After the vows were exchanged and they were pronounced man and wife, Jason turned her, lifted her veil and said, "God, you are beautiful. You take my breath away, wife. I love you."

"I love you too, husband," Abby said.

Then she smiled, stood on tip toes and kissed him, as everyone applauded.

"We finally made it, babe! You are all mine," Jason said to her.

"And you are all mine," Abby replied.

Music was played. Dancing was done. Food and drink were shared by all. Someone stood up and shouted, "Hey Jason, when are you going to let us dance with the bride?" Everyone started in with the "Yeah! Give her up, Jason, we get to have a dance!"

"Well, babe, it looks like I have to share you with your minions," Jason said to Abby.

Then he took her hand and led her to the center of the yard to have the first dance with her. Next came Leo, he tapped Jason on the shoulder.

"Okay brother, my turn."

Jason placed her hand into Leo's.

While Leo danced with her, he said, "Sis, you are absolutely beautiful. You look like a princess. Are you as happy as you look?"

"I couldn't be happier. I think my heart's going to burst," she said to him.

She wrapped her arms around her twin brother's neck, and kissed his cheek.

Leo felt a tap on his shoulder. It was Jacob.

"Move aside, son. Time for me to dance with my daughter."

Leo took her hand and placed it into Jacobs. Jacob whisked her away with some pretty fancy moves that made her laugh.

"Sweetheart, we are so happy you came into our son's life. You saved him. We haven't seen him this happy since I don't know when. You are family now, and if you ever need anything, I expect you to come to us. We love you, Abby," Jacob said, and he kissed her cheek.

She looked up at him as tears ran down her cheeks.

"Thank you....Dad," she said, and smiled up at him.

He gave her a hug and got tapped on the shoulder.

Everyone there took their turn to dance with the bride, but when Jason saw how tired she was getting, he swept her up in his arms and ran into the house with her.

"Thank you for the rest," Abby said.

Jason removed her shoes and gave her a foot massage,

while she sat on the couch for a few minutes.

"I'm your knight in shining armor, remember?" Jason said, smiling at her.

Just then, Debbie came in telling her that it was time for the bouquet toss, and she had to get back outside.

When it came time for the bouquet toss, all the women formed behind Abby. She gave it a high toss and it hit Debbie in the head accidentally. She grabbed it and tossed it to Renee and said, while laughing, "You're next!"

Jason had Abby sat on a chair as all the men gathered around. He slowly lifted her gown, and the men started whistling. He pulled the garter off her thigh, stood up, and shot it straight to Leo.

"Just you wait. You better make me best man because pay back's a bitch!" Jason said, laughing at him.

After Jason and Abby smeared wedding cake all over each other's faces, they went inside long enough to change into travel clothes. When they returned, everyone greeted them with hugs and kisses, and wished them a good time on the honeymoon.

Leo approached them and said, "Are you two love birds ready to go? You don't want to miss your flight. Renee and I are taking you to the airport."

"Abby, I packed your bags. They are in the truck along with Jason's bags. Have fun my sister," Debbie said, and gave her a huge hug.

They waved good bye to everyone then headed to the car.

Once inside the car, Renee said, "Debbie packed your bags, but I packed a tote bag for you filled with crackers, your pre-natal pills and vitamins, and a few other things to help you stay healthy and safe," Renee said, and gave her a wink.

As they pulled out of the driveway Jason said to Abby, "It is just you and me and our baby for the next few weeks, Mrs. Donahue."

"I like the sound of that, Mr. Donahue," Abby said with a grin.

"Leo, you have our itinerary and all my cell numbers. Call if it is necessary, otherwise.....," Jason said.

"Jason, I have it covered. You just have a good time and take care of my sister," Leo said, as they drove away.

A dark van with two men inside watched as they passed.

"Did you plant the tracers?" said the one behind the wheel.

"One on her luggage and one on his. I put them inside the linings."

"That should be plenty," the driver said.

"Good. No one fucks with the family, and gets away with it!"

The two men looked forward and watched as the truck went down the street and out of sight.

ABOUT THE AUTHOR

Addie Herrington resides in the suburbs of Pittsburgh, Pennsylvania, with her husband, Jim, and their collie dog, Leo. She enjoys getting lost in a good book but craves getting into the "zone" when writing. Having the "empty nest" allows for a bunch of zoning.

Addie has done everything from being a cabbie, to being a cashier, to working in a labor gang, to working on an aircraft, to being in the medical field in different capacities. She was an EMT, medical technician, a vet tech, and a caregiver. She has three adult children, Bryan, Brett, and Ashley. Now that her children are grown and have lives of their own, she is taking her turn to finish her books.

Made in United States
North Haven, CT
09 June 2023

37570977R10114